I0591711

The Big One

Patrick Barb

Anuci Press

First paperback edition 2025

Anuci Press edition 2025

www.anuci-press.com

Cover Design by Lynne Hansen

ISBN 979-8-9989778-4-8 (paperback)

ISBN 979-8-9989778-5-5(eBook)

THE BIG ONE

PATRICK BARB

Chapter 1

Someone dying wasn't a reason to celebrate. Hank knew that.

And yet, when the last call of the day ended up being an O.D. in the Haight, with cops and the city's overworked medical examiners swarming a filthy single-occupancy apartment, the resulting relief was unavoidable.

After Vic and Darren were waved back into the ambulance and their three-person crew was told to go *home*, Hank revved the engine and flicked on both lights and siren.

Darren made his way up from the back, pushing against the seatbacks and sliding over the center console like a gymnast on a pommel horse. Landing in the front passenger seat, he turned to Hank and said, "You know you're only supposed to turn those on for an emergency, right?"

The way he said it—deadpan, with a hint of concern at the end—made Hank turn his head. But the driver rolled his eyes and huffed out an exasperated breath when he caught the shit-eating grin on his co-worker's face.

"You fuck," Hank said.

Darren exploded with laughter.

In the back, Vic stretched her seatbelt across her stout upper body and clicked it in place. Her hand, with concealer worn away to reveal many self-inflicted scars, hovered above her pants' pocket. Hank watched from the rearview. He knew she sometimes brought a flask on the job. He hoped she didn't have it and wouldn't take a drink from it if she did. Even though their shift was over, one more infraction while in the ambulance and he'd have to report her to the hospital administrators.

And that was the absolute last thing Vic needed.

When she pulled her empty hand back and laid it across her lap, Hank breathed a sigh of relief. With that mini-crisis averted, he slammed on the brakes, sending Darren—who still hadn't buckled up—headbanging into the dashboard. "Man!" the gangly man shouted, palms slapping the glovebox.

This time, Hank laughed. A single sharp *HA!*

As if to say, *NOW, we're even.*

Giving the driver side-eye, Darren clicked his seatbelt in at last. Hank's foot bounced on the gas pedal in anticipation of the trip home.

"What's the hurry?" Darren asked.

"Sitter's leaving soon. Gotta get back to take Marcy and Abel out for ice cream. I promised 'em," Hank said.

"Oooh, look at Mister Mom here taking the kids out for ice cream. Whatchoo gonna have, man?"

Vic chimed in from the back. "Butter pecan?"

"Naw, naw, my man's gonna have himself some rocky road..."

Hank's answer came as a mumble, tone modulated so the others wouldn't hear.

He should've known what a bad idea *that* was. Like throwing chum for sharks. Would've been better to say nothing at all.

Darren leaned to the left, pushing his shoulder against the driver's. "Excuse me? What was that, senōr?"

Hank sighed. "I'm not having any. Trying to watch what I eat..."

Ever the shark, Darren attacked fast. He grabbed the white uniform shirt covering Hank's stomach. Gave his belly a good jiggle.

"Awww, buddy, ain't gonna lose the muffin top though, are ya? That's your moneymaker, bay-bee."

Hank grabbed Darren's hand. Pushed it away. "You asshol—"

He bit off his rejoinder. Without warning, his stomach flip-flopped with its acrobatics matched by the steering wheel sliding sharply from side to side, rubbing hard at the tan skin of Hank's palms.

"Pull over!" Vic shouted from the back.

She didn't need to tell Hank twice. He wrestled control of the vehicle back from the rattling tremors shaking the ambulance and its passengers. He aimed for the nearest bit of available curb. By the sound of honking horns, screeching brakes, and what might've been the tinkling of broken headlights falling on asphalt, it seemed every other driver had the same idea.

The trio braced for impact. No one *said* the word. But they were damn sure all thinking it...

Earthquake.

Except, what came next wasn't the typical early morning rumbler, the kind Hank and the others were accustomed to, the small price to pay for living in the Bay Area. It wasn't a minor tremor, where a lamp falls over or a few wine glasses shatter. The initial rumble that sent the ambulance off the road was a mere amuse-bouche compared to the sumptuous main course of mass destruction that followed.

First, there was nothing. But a bad nothing, accompanied by unease and a certainty that the worst was yet to come.

And come it did.

The earth exploded as though it were a shaken can of soda stabbed with a Bowie knife at maximum pressure. The ground cracked open ahead of them. One minute the road and surrounding scenery were whole, maybe a pothole here or there, a piece of gum stuck to a sidewalk, and then...

A loud cracking followed, the way thunder trails lightning. The sound alone made Hank nauseous. He clapped his hands over his ears and moaned softly. The splintering earth reminded him of feet stomping dry leaves in a New England autumn pastoral. This strange sense-memory flung him back to childhood travels East, and visits to his Gramamaw's for Christmas.

The rending of rock, asphalt, and concrete was more intense. Like the tread of a giant—some fairy tale ogre come to life—trampling the earth and leaving its mark across great swaths of civilization.

The jagged tear split the street ahead of the ambulance and surged forward, backward, sideways, everywhere and anywhere all at once.

"What's happening? What's going on?" Vic asked from her inconvenient spot in the back.

"You'll see soon!" Darren shouted.

And he was right, as the tremors continued and the resulting shockwaves brought the damage past the ambulance.

"Hold on!" Hank cried, taking his own advice as he gripped the steering wheel tighter. Asphalt and concrete rolled under them like choppy sea waves. Up and down, up and down.

Darren wasn't laughing anymore. Instead, he whispered prayers under his breath. Enough *Dios mio's* and *Madre Maria's* to go around.

When Hank checked the mirror, he saw Vic's mouth turned shiny. Droplets of brown liquid beaded at the corners of her lips. Her eyes met Hank's, pleading. *Please don't tell anyone what I've done.*

Hank returned a smile that probably appeared more like a grimace given their ongoing circumstances and his accompanying confusion and uncertainty. But it was the best assurance he could offer her.

With his heart beating and his stomach continuing its internal gymnastics, it was a moment before Hank realized the tremors had subsided. The sudden squawk of the radio managed to scare everyone inside the ambulance, more than the immense quake they'd just survived had.

"Ambulance 7, do you copy?" a disembodied, extremely agitated voice asked through the roaring static.

Hank clicked on the two-way. "Copy, dispatch, Ambulance 7 here. How're y'all doing over there?"

There was a long pause and then, "Not great. We could use you all back here..."

Darren reached over and shook Hank's shoulder. "Hank! Hank! Look!"

Hank did. Letting the two-way cord droop in his hand, like a wilted rose, he peered across through the front passenger window, following Darren's finger.

He did so in the nick of time. From the curb where they'd parked to the liquor store—QUAN'S DISCOUNT LIQUORS AND WINE—was probably about a foot. Through the now open-air front of the building, thanks to the shattered plate glass all around, the driver and EMT observed screaming, crying patrons and shop employees, each person covered in glass shards. Some of the slivers cut into flesh, glass from the store windows but also from smashed bottles, glistening with liquor and the deep burgundy reds of wine.

Hank shook his head. The scene was like something from a medieval illustration of Hell, with glass-studded, bleeding wretches begging for mercy. He whispered a prayer of his own. Then, a low moan emanated from underground, a giant awakening below the liquor store.

One second, the store was standing, damaged but present. Then, the ground, just one foot from the ambulance, cratered and the resulting sinkhole swallowed QUAN'S LIQUORS AND WINE like a gluttonous Fourth of July hot-dog-eating contestant. Bloody, glass-scored survivors and all.

"Fucking drive!" Vic hiccoughed from the back. The zig-zag fissure, racing across the sidewalk from the sinkhole, headed straight for the ambulance. Its movement compelled Darren to join the chorus.

"Drive! Drive! Drive!"

Hank pulled forward, the front of the ambulance knocking over a shiny, barely-used Harley Davidson that probably belonged to some tech bro. He wrenched the steering wheel hard to the left, smashing into a stroller left abandoned and empty (*God Hank hoped it was empty*) in the middle of the road. Then, he drove.

Sirens wailed. Flashing red and white lights spilled across crumbling buildings, electrical fires burning unchecked, and all the dead and dying people kept out of sight.

Inside his head, Hank's panicked screaming continued unfettered. When that stopped, he started repeating the names of his kids. Over and over again.

Marcy, Abel, Marcy, Abel, Marcy, Abel...

He wouldn't, *couldn't* allow himself to picture their faces. He knew if he did, the chances of imagining the carnage spread across the Bay to their apartment complex would be too strong. He couldn't go on if he managed to envision their sweet light brown faces buried under brick and steel, plastic and glass. It would be too much to bear.

Even as he sped toward the hospital, his whispered words struck the windshield. Not a prayer, but a promise.

"Daddy's coming home."

Chapter 2

The two men and one woman sat in the ambulance, each puzzling over the answer to the unexpected question before them: how could an entire hospital *disappear* in broad daylight?

Of course, at a physical level, Hank and the others understood what'd happened. Moments prior, they'd pulled up short of the massive sinkhole where their hospital and surrounding buildings had stood a mere hour earlier when they'd gone for their final call of the day. After reversing ever so carefully and taking more time than a near-sighted blue hair to execute a Y-turn from the edge of the pit, Hank and his two co-workers climbed carefully from their vehicle to assess the situation.

Hank thought he was ready for whatever sights might wait past the rim of the sinkhole. He'd had two tours of duty as an M1 armor crewman driving a tank in Afghanistan under his belt, then five years behind an ambulance in one of the major metropolitan cities of the West Coast. He knew from injuries, minor and massive, and he'd seen death up-close and personal more times than he cared to share.

But the wreckage of San Francisco Uptown General showcased destruction and death at Costco-sized proportions. The crater spread across several city blocks, just as the hospital once had. Steel, concrete, glass, and plastic, none of the building materials were spared from the damage. The hungry earth had ripped away everything that was built on top of it.

Sewer lines leading to the site must've burst from multiple impacts since the sinkhole was filled with blackened water sloshing through the shattered ruins. The buildings had crumpled into each other like a collapsed house of cards. Brackish wastewater flowed between the debris, adding an otherworldly appearance to the damage site. It was like the crew had stumbled upon the sunken remnants of an ancient civilization reclaimed by the sea.

But there was no marble-columned temple, no row of terra cotta statues, or ruler's gilded coffin waiting below their feet. Instead, they found a twenty-first-century, state-of-the-art hospital leveled in an instant with no regard for the purpose it served, the good it provided, or the people inside. Given the function of the structure, not only was there flooding, but electrical fires danced across the water in a blue-green flaming pattern like frost on windshields writ large...larger than Hank, Darren, or Vic could conceive.

Still, Vic tried to put words to the tableau. "All those people. The children's wing...doctors, nurses..."

Darren turned away, dropped to his knees, and vomited up the meatball sub he'd scarfed on their last break—an event that felt like several lifetimes ago. He didn't bother wiping his mouth when he finished. Instead, he let orange spittle strands dangle from his bottom lip.

Hank said nothing. He hardly moved.

The hole was so big, like a meteor had struck the Earth. Like the monster asteroid that wiped out the dinosaurs had come back for more, plummeted down from space and striking in the middle of San Francisco.

All around the trio, alarms blared. Screams echoed off those few buildings still standing...for the moment. Hank was certain some of the cries for help came from below their feet. Those voices of the damned urged whoever heard them to come closer. But to do so would mean the destruction of the listener as well.

It was all Hank could do to tear himself away. With a bellowing cry, tears running down his cheeks, he turned from the crater. Heavy stomping feet crushed ruined asphalt into black crumbs under his heels as he made for the idling ambulance.

Behind him, Darren rose to his feet and took Vic by the elbow. When they got to the ambulance, Hank was already in the driver's seat, ready to leave. However, he hadn't closed the driver's side door yet, so the EMTs had a small window in which to act.

Darren, finally wiping away his vomit, spread his befouled hand across his uniform shirt. "What's next, buddy?" he asked.

"I'm gonna go to Oakland." Hank shot a sharp-edged look at Darren and Vic, daring them to say something in response.

But his glare softened when he found no resistance forthcoming. Darren simply nodded and walked to the front passenger side. Likewise, Vic went to the back and pulled the doors open. She hoisted herself up and removed the flask from her pocket. Hank pulled his door shut and Darren did the same on his side. Vic guzzled caramel-colored liquid from the flask's tiny metal hole before taking her seat. Neither of her co-workers appeared to give much of a shit.

Darren waited until Vic finished her swallow before he held his hand out. When the silver flask came around to Hank, he demurred. "Gotta drive," he said.

"You're sure about getting to Oakland?" Vic asked from the back. Her voice was a husky rasp. On days devoid of natural disasters, Darren used to joke about Vic making more money doing phone sex work. She'd roll her eyes and shoot back, "How do you know I'm not?"

Hank missed those days already.

In place of a time machine to return to that unblemished period, Hank focused on navigating through the crisis at hand. He pointed to the radio, already tuned to the news channel. A droning NPR anchor pronounced each word from Emergency Services, slow and steady, as though they might break—or break *her*—at the slightest pressure. She made note of minimal damage across the bay in Oakland and Emeryville. Then, she expounded on the reported damage in San Francisco before moving to reports out of southern California, scant as those were.

Everything the newsreader said about the lower portion of the state came in the past tense. *Los Angeles was... Residents of Orange County were believed to be all... No one in Hollywood was expected to...*

Hank rubbed his kneecap, feeling as though he'd lost a limb. Suddenly, the unfathomable loss of life in the hospital crater became a community theater performance of disaster in comparison to what was reported by that monotone news drone. Whatever sobs she might've produced were apparently swallowed off-mic.

"Holy shit, man. It's the big one." If Darren expected a response from his companions, then, perhaps their non-reactions would've disappointed him. But they were all three professionals, with a combined twenty-five years of experience in serving the dead and dying. So, Hank let the words slide past. For her part, Vic fumbled with her seatbelt, staring at the medical equipment across from her with a dull, glassy-eyed expression.

Hank put the ambulance back into drive and repeated his earlier assertion. "We're going to Oakland. I can get us there. I can find a way."

Darren was a long-time bachelor, and Vic was fresh from her third failed marriage. "But hopefully third successful divorce," she'd said deadpan in those hours before their worlds collapsed.

Neither of the EMTs had anyone waiting for them at their respective homes. If they even had homes to return *to*. But Hank did. Marcy and Abel: the smiling, dimple-faced ten and seven-year-old girl and boy whose department store portrait wallet print picture he kept clipped to the visor every shift. Hank's little rebellion against the ambulance corps' rules.

"Okay, dog," Darren said, "You got the wheel. Let's go save those kiddos."

Chapter 3

Darren flipped the radio dial back and forth, checking each station on the FM *and* AM bands with a shifting frequency that revealed no discernable pattern. Sometimes Hank had him switch away mid-sentence even as the president's spokesperson expressed concern about the loss of life and property, other times they'd leave static roaring in their ears like so much white noise for long, ever-expanding minutes.

Hank's focus was laser sharp. He knew what information he needed. While his body focused on the task at hand, a small part of his mind retreated to the desert. He was back following orders in a convoy of hot-blooded American freedom. When he was there, he'd always kept his eyes open. His ears as well. After all, that one glint of light, one sound, one word, might prove the difference between reaching your destination intact or never showing up alive anywhere ever again.

He listened for road closures, detours, and delays, all while inching the ambulance forward and waiting patiently within slower-moving lanes of traffic when necessary. When a break appeared, Hank's foot slid to the gas. The ambulance shot forward, balanced on the near fluid shifting tectonic plates underneath its tires. Like mercury floating in water inside an old thermometer.

When he wasn't working the radio, Darren provided running commentary on the sights surrounding them. Hank let him ramble on. After all, Darren's words were more grist for the mill. More information to filter. It was Darren who noted when a swath of sidewalk cleared, providing an alternate route around a three-car pile-up.

Past the hospital sinkhole, other people wandered amid the rubble on unsteady, trauma-shaken legs. The visible bodies stretched across the debris were beyond any assistance the medics might render. Hank tried not to think about the people they *couldn't* see. The people inside the smoking craters, rubble mountain ranges, and the disaster scenes that resembled an alien landscape of aluminum foil, pipe cleaners, and blood. Dwelling on them too long would lead to a breakdown. And Hank didn't have time to lose it, not when so much depended on him.

Not when his whole world depended on him. A whole world in two smiling faces.

His hands itched against the steering wheel, alive with a sensation akin to fire ants crawling over his knuckles from *inside* his skin. His legs tingled as well, powered by the phantom buzzing of a cell phone he'd left back in his locker at the hospital. He'd stored it there as a precaution. After all, the last thing he wanted was to lose his phone while out on a call and be unable to tell the kids he was on his way home.

"Or you could lose it in the pits of Hell…"

Vic's muttered words came as a harsh blow, breaking Hank's concentration.

"What's that, Victoria?" he asked.

But when he checked the back, the sloshed EMT's head tilted to the side, her mouth hanging open. Her nostrils flared as she snored. Her brow was wrinkled. Hank found it appropriate. *Even if she could sleep through the end of the world, it's not like she has to be at peace about it.*

In the driver's seat, Hank pinched the bridge of his nose. Closing his eyes for a moment.

"Hank!"

At Darren's cry, he opened them again, hoping he hadn't made a fatal mistake.

In front of the ambulance, a mob of blood-streaked survivors smashed out the windows of a station wagon parked at an angle against the curb. Hank stomped on the brakes. Flipped off the siren and the lights. Tires skidded against the crushed asphalt. One of the station wagon attackers turned to stare down Hank and Darren. This large man, with purple-black bags under his eyes, stared first at the driver, then turned his attention to Darren. Glass from the punched-out station wagon window studded the big man's fists as he held them up. He appeared as a child offering a finger painting for his parents' smiling approval.

Hank didn't wait for Darren's assessment of the situation. His right hand dropped to the gear shift, and he threw the ambulance in reverse, backing up to get a little clearance, before exploding forward like a bullet. Something heavy thumped against Darren's side of the vehicle and the EMT swore. "Shit!"

His mirror was shattered, a spider web of cracks enveloping the glass.

Some of the mob broke away from the station wagon and chased after the ambulance on foot. However, Hank felt confident there was enough open roadway ahead that he'd put considerable distance between the crazies and the vehicle. What upset him more was the figure he noticed being dragged, kicking and thrashing, out of the station wagon, by those who remained behind.

He'd assumed the attackers were merely looters, desperate people trying to snag whatever goods might've been left behind. He was sure that couldn't have been a person they were going after. It just didn't make sense. After all, Hank had lived through any number of life-or-death situations and always found people to be more inclined to preserve life when given the option.

But what he'd seen back at that station wagon...

Chapter 4

The aftershocks slowed and more people emerged onto the streets, crawling from the semi-stable wreckage, stumbling through the rubble of ruined lives. Each new mob spotted wandering the broken streets and sidewalks appeared similar in make-up and mood to the one the ambulance had escaped. Everyone was angry, raging. As though the earthquakes were an affront to their reality that they would *not* tolerate.

In the back of the ambulance, Vic sobbed. She had her cell phone out and was trying the numbers of various ex-lovers with no luck.

"You're gonna run out of battery if you keep using it like that," Darren said.

"Shut up!" Vic's face flushed red, and her eyes were rheumy with a watery mustard yellow highlighted by her burst blood vessels.

Hank's foot moved to the brake, but he resisted the urge to stop. The reports on the radio came more and more sporadically; but from what he gathered, it appeared as though the new Bay Bridge remained intact. They had someone on-air who claimed to have made it across.

The updates she provided to the host started fairly normal in their content and delivery. "We gunned it across, didn't stop for anything..."

But when the woman was asked about the presence of other survivors on the bridge, she took a hard swallow before launching into an expletive-filled rambling rant about crab-fish-people. "The claws...they scraped the door, ripped out the back...my sister...she was huddled there with our cat...they took her onto the bridge. Then, they smeared her across the road, like...before they dove over the side...the water's red. It's all fucking red and foaming!"

The host stopped the call there. "Sorry about that folks, technical difficulties."

Hank snorted. *Technical difficulties, my ass.*

Ahead, a ravaged MUNI bus stretched across the intersection with jagged asphalt cracked into a vertical spike of ebony severing the vehicle through its accordioned middle. Hank ran calculations in the seconds passing between catching sight of the obstruction and his vehicle's barreling approach.

He'd driven a tank through narrow market streets with pissed-off villagers throwing rocks, rotten fruit, and invective his way. *And sometimes bullets and rockets.* He'd crossed semi-mountainous terrain weaving his death machine around boulders and debris, across gashes in the earth. Of course, the difference then was that he knew Marcy and Abel were home while he did *that* driving. They were safe. He had no doubt about it.

He took his eyes off the path ahead for a moment, a microsecond. Just long enough to look back at Vic, cradling her phone. She pet it like a newborn pup, wet and whimpering, extracted from its mother.

"Hank, watch out!"

At Darren's exclamation, Hank felt control of the vehicle ripped away from him. As his focus returned, he noted Darren's hands on the wheel, yanking the vehicle to the side. Before a "whatthehell" could even trip off Hank's tongue and past his lips, the ambulance veered to the side, headed straight for a fiery slag heap of metal that might've once been a mailbox. Only then, did Hank finally notice the bleeding man standing in the road. Waiting for them.

Chapter 5

Even with the brake pressed down, his foot sitting heavy on the molded metallic pad, and the ambulance parked, Hank still experienced the sensation of his body traveling forward at great speeds, pushing the seatbelt deep into his chest—even though there was no such movement of man or restraint. To counteract this imagined force, Hank pressed himself back against the seat, as though a giant hand had smashed through the front windshield, flexing long fingers, before pinning him in place. His ears rang with the imagined tinkling of shattered glass, like church bells on Christmas morning. More crying seemed an inevitable by-product of this condition. But even as the first fat tear sat full and sparkling on Hank's lower lash, the Bleeding Man stood unmoving in his peripheral.

Even as the ambulance shrieked to a halt mere feet away, the Bleeding Man hadn't moved from his spot near the intersection. The smoking ruin of the bus served as backdrop for whatever bloody one-man show the injured stranger might see fit to put up for his captive audience.

To call the man injured was putting it lightly. First, he was coated in a thick, tacky film of red. Unmistakably blood, and yet so much of the life-giving substance as to appear absurd. For a moment, Hank wondered if the stranger might've doused himself in cans of tomato soup to ward off a skunk's stench instead. Having that amount of blood on the outside of a person's body, and to have that person still be standing as though nothing was wrong, it didn't add up. Looking closer, twisting in his seat for a better view of the Bleeding Man, Hank observed nicks, cuts, and scratches across the man's bare chest. His aquamarine blue pajama pants sported purple spots where blood had cascaded down and dried on thin cloth.

It disgusted Hank to see so much bloody skin, including the man's bare feet, pebbled in asphalt and granite chunks and splashing in jammy puddles of blood. Hank coughed, forcing down the bile that made its way up his esophagus. He had to remind himself that he'd seen so much worse overseas. Hell, he'd seen so much worse earlier in the week when they'd treated a three-year-old who'd taken a bullet to the face, tearing off an ear and blinding the child in his ruined right eye.

But this was different somehow.

There, in the middle of the intersection, before the hollowed-out and empty shell of the city bus, the Bleeding Man took no outward notice of his injuries. They were an accepted part of his being. And that was what upset Hank, what turned his stomach.

Worst of all, though, was the man's left arm. It hung limp, all stretched and reddened by burst, oozing blood vessels. Torn ligaments exposed both hamburger-striated flesh and gray bone, transforming the corpse-pale arm into a floppy worm of an appendage. The wrist was turned the wrong way around so that the front of the hand was open toward the ambulance, both palm and elbow pointing forward at the same time.

Darren's clapping hands freed Hank from his traumatized contemplation of the Bleeding Man. "Let's go," the EMT said, crawling over the center console to join Vic in the back of the ambulance.

As he stood straight on top of the console, his head nearly touching the roof and one hand resting on Hank's shoulder, Darren whistled, aiming to get Vic's attention, rousing her from drunken slumber. Hank reached behind him and grabbed Darren. "Wait," he said.

Darren tried to pull away and continue toward the back of the vehicle. But Hank wasn't having it. He held on tight.

"What're you doing?" Hank asked.

"We've gotta try and help," Darren said, his features softening from the initial annoyance that crossed his visage when Hank first grabbed him.

For his part, Hank hesitated. Vic was slowly stirring, already unbuckling her seatbelt and trying to pretend like she hadn't been passed out the whole time. The ambulance driver returned his attention to the Bleeding Man. Hank had witnessed incidents where adrenaline and fear helped someone keep going even when afflicted with mortal injuries. A twenty-something-year-old soldier left as nothing more than a spine and a head yet still managing to mumble out his last words—that was one of things that finally brought him home for good.

But the Bleeding Man wasn't that. Hank didn't have words for what he was.

"My kids..."

He did have *those* words.

Marcy and Abel: they were what made sense to Hank. And so, they were what he fell back to.

But Hank's moment of hesitation was all Darren needed. The EMT pulled free from his grasp and jumped to the back. "Vic, prep for triage," he ordered, striding past her and continuing to the street.

Vic nodded. "Yep, yep, I can do it."

It sounded as though she were trying to convince herself.

Darren called back to the front of the ambulance. "We'll get your kids, Hank. But we can't leave people to suffer along the way. Not when they're right in our faces."

Then, he moved toward the intersection.

He approached the Bleeding Man slowly, carefully. His hands were raised with his palms out, in an attempt to show the wounded man that he wasn't a threat.

Hank gripped the steering wheel tight. In doing so, he thought about his co-worker's—his friend's—parting words. *We can't just leave people to suffer along the way.*

Except that's just it. That Bleeding Man doesn't look like he's suffering. There's something in his eyes there. It almost looks like he enjoys it.

Chapter 6

The rogue Ambulance 7 continued its journey to the Bay Bridge. Except where there was once a crew of three, now a fourth member had joined their ensemble. The patient. The injured. The Bleeding Man. He hadn't given a name—hadn't said anything—since being led onboard by Vic and Darren, so Hank had taken to calling the man as he saw him.

The Bleeding Man. Like the name of some off-brand Boogeyman of urban legend. Or from one of those creepypasta stories Marcy had recently discovered and liked scaring Abel with. Livia would've chastised him about letting her read if his wife were still around to do such reprimanding.

Except, she wasn't around. Hadn't been for a long time. Even if some days still felt like the day after her death, even all those years later.

The Bleeding Man sat on the bench across from Vic as she scrolled through numbers on her phone.

"SF General, Mission...no answers there. I dunno if the lines are even up and working," she said.

"Doesn't matter," Hank called from the driver's seat. "Can't see a good route to get to either of 'em."

"What about Kentwood?"

"Are you fucking serious?" Darren asked, turning around in his seat and glaring at Vic like she'd insulted his mother. "Kentwood's back the way we came."

Hank took one hand off the steering wheel and moved it toward his friend to defuse this sudden outburst. "Easy there," he said.

Darren snorted, elbowing Hank's offered hand away. He pointed to the front windshield. As if to say, *You, focus on driving.*

From the back, Vic whispered an apology. "I'm sorry, I'm just trying to help."

Darren's reactions, his hair-trigger temper, none of it mapped to the happy-go-lucky, gallows'-humor-spouting Darren from most of the shifts Hank had driven. There was a mean, nasty edge to this Darren's words, to his movements, to the very way he sat in the passenger seat and scratched at the stubble on his cheeks and down his neck.

Still, Hank supposed he had a point. Kentwood *was* back near the Haight. Not a great suggestion from Vic to say the least.

Even still, once it was mentioned, the driver couldn't get the clinic's name out of his head. "Kentwood...Kentwood..."

Some revelatory insight appeared poised to break through, yet it wasn't quite ready to make itself known.

Hank would've kept that name rolling over and over, again and again, in his head. Except for what the Bleeding Man did next.

Chapter 7

Inside the womb of the Life-Giving Whore
In the rocky embrace of her fiery core
He's slumbered long, we've forgotten his face
The One from Before and After this race
Men, women, children, living, and dead
All come to serve below his tentacled head...

Those verses were the last words Hank recognized as English spewing from the black-licorice-colored lips of the Bleeding Man.

Without warning, the stranger had stood up from the bench, seeming to snap the restraints Darren and Vic had locked into place to prevent further injury. The Bleeding Man shrugged off the leather straps as if they were gossamer threads. Then, he began his sermon.

The roads were getting tighter. More rubble and debris, more abandoned vehicles, more of the angry, howling mobs who seemed to have forsaken any notion of helping their fellow humans and who instead seemed committed to a shared goal of tearing down whatever the earthquake and its aftershocks hadn't already demolished. Given the difficulty of navigating through this hellscape, Hank had to trust Vic to be a professional and do her job like he damn well knew she could.

After all, they'd handled tweakers, meth-heads, coked-up Triad members in Chinatown, and any number of dangerous, uncooperative patients before. The Bleeding Man shouldn't have been anything new.

Still, brief glimpses in the rearview offered a staccato vision of a nightmare brought to life. The Bleeding Man's eyes rolled back white, and his tongue moved in lapping waves against the roof of his mouth and his bottom lip, producing an ululating series of unrecognizable syllables. Something between the croaking rasps of toads in a swamp and an ancient civilization's harsh intonations, something from the first scraping, scrabbling attempts at language.

"Suh-sir. Sir? You need to take a seat, sir." That was Vic, trying to stay calm. Trying to remain a professional.

In the passenger seat beside Hank, Darren's hand moved to his belt. His fingers stopped above the release. Hank was all set for Darren to hop back and restrain the Bleeding Man. Maybe put him in a chokehold and make a quip about Vic owing him a date. All so she could fire back, "You're not enough of a pussy to be my type." And then the tension would break, and everything would return to normal.

But that wasn't the kind of day the crew of Ambulance 7 was having.

When the Bleeding Man lifted his injured arm, it snapped into place like a fishing pole when something's taken the bait at the end of the line. The crack of bone and the slippery release of wet flesh followed. Strands of muscled tissue hung dripping and blood-soaked from his arm.

That alone should've been enough. The gruesome injury—its appearance, its sound, even the coppery smell of blood—should've been enough.

And yet, the Bleeding Man was just getting started.

From outside the ambulance, the growing mob hooted and hollered, dancing and darting between cars. Hank knew the road required his attention. The last thing he saw in the rearview was the Bleeding Man's face, his mouth opened to let strips of his own ruined arm flesh fill him.

Eyes back on the road, Hank drove to the sounds of chewing. And Vic was gagging, trying against all odds to find her voice again.

"Oh God."

At Vic's bile-choked exclamation, it was as if the mob of survivors outside could hear the goings-on in the ambulance, like her minor blasphemy was a Bat-signal, drawing their attention to the rescue vehicle's creeping progress. Two SUVS left abandoned on either side of an intersection, having nearly collided, provided a narrow path forward for Hank. He steeled himself, said a prayer—not to God, but to Marcy and Abel back home in Oakland—then he floored it.

The scrape and whine of metal and glass colliding came with a nails-on-chalkboard intensity. A roar from the wandering survivors echoed above the ruins as the ambulance pushed the abandoned cars aside and knocked one mirror each from both vehicles. The ambulance's side mirrors remained intact. Strong.

Hank sighed with relief, but the feeling evaporated like the last drop of canteen water in the desert. The acceleration and impact from the collision with the two SUVs had knocked both Vic and the Bleeding Man off-balance. Soon enough, something wet dribbled onto Hank's shoulder, staining the white of his shirt a bruised cherry. Glancing back, he found the white eyes of the Bleeding Man and a mouth of chewed-up, but not-yet-swallowed flesh. The lips moved, as the Bleeding Man talked with his mouth full.

Hank didn't have time for whatever message the Bleeding Man was trying to convey. He lifted his arm, lining up his elbow before driving it back, hard as he could. He felt the wet crunch of bone and cartilage traveling up his forearm, making his fingers tingle. A new outlet for blood loss presented itself to the Bleeding Man.

Hank hoped the blow would send the Bleeding Man reeling. He wanted the stranger to fall into Vic's arms, so she could put a choke-hold on the man, and they could...deal with him. But Vic was on the floor, still trying to get back to her feet. Even with the adrenaline, no doubt pumping through her body, her earlier drinking appeared to still be taking its toll.

The Bleeding Man's mouth was full of blood and snot, lips smack-ing together as he laughed. He didn't fall, even with the explosive force behind Hank's blow. The all-whites of his eyes provided no answers, no more than they were a window into his soul. *If he had any soul at all.* But his laughing smile spoke volumes.

Instead of falling to the back, he lunged to the side. Grasping onto Darren's seat, as if it were a life buoy thrown amid a turbulent, raging sea. Fists beat against the ambulance from outside. A tribal rhythm tattooed against the slowed-down vehicle. Hands pressed against the glass on the driver's side door. Then, a face smacked hard into it. Not enough to dent or break the glass, but enough to make Hank jump in his seat and curse.

He was back in the desert. Back in a market turned hostile, the only route of escape was through.

"Forgive me," he said and gunned it.

Hank hoped against hope that the crunching sounds following came from the destroyed roadway, bits of churned-up rock and as-phalt, and not from breaking bones.

The ambulance bumped up onto a curb, then back to the street, then up again. Turning corners, shooting across a green space with the earth overturned and muddy. Splattered brown soil covered the white paint of the vehicle's exterior. On and on, Hank drove with single-minded purpose until the moment when he looked in the side mirror and there was no one close. Distant bedraggled figures limped behind in the vehicle's wake.

Again, Hank performed the mental calculations, assessing their best options for survival. He put the vehicle in park, practically busting out of the restraining seatbelt across his chest and lap when the wheels stopped.

He barreled toward the back, knocking the Bleeding Man away from Darren. For his part, Darren remained seated, his back pressed against the faux leather seat. Eyes forward. His mouth, a thin, silent dash.

Hank didn't have time to consider why the other man hadn't fought back. Or how he'd let the Bleeding Man hang over his shoulder like a pitch-fork-wielding devil in a cartoon offering unsolicited bad advice, urging the sinner onto the worst decisions possible. There was no time for those thoughts, as he let his momentum carry him to the next point of conflict.

Hands slicked with blood that wasn't his but still holding tight to the Bleeding Man's shirt, Hank's feet moved until they struck the back doors of the ambulance. The impact sent mini-tremors echoing across Hank's arms. "Vic!" he cried out, hoping she'd been able to get it together enough to stand, to move.

Yes, indeed.

She was there beside him, somewhat unsteady. But standing.

"Open the door!"

The Bleeding Man finally squirmed in Hank's grasp. It wasn't that he was stronger than the ex-soldier. Far from it. Hank's arms and hands were close to the size of the Bleeding Man's mid-section after all. The danger came from the blood, the slick, hot, sticky coating that meant the ambulance driver had to put his full concentration to the task of holding the Bleeding Man in place.

Vic's hands moved like an aged fighter's. Trying to find when to jab. But instead of a blow, she waited until the silver handles of the door were available. A twist and a push. Then, they opened.

Hank acted fast, shoving the Bleeding Man out of the ambulance and onto the ruined asphalt. It took everything to let go in time, to make sure momentum didn't send him flying out of the vehicle as well.

But when it counted, Vic was there.

She wrapped her arms around Hank, and they fell back into the vehicle's now-violated interior. The rattling shook loose equipment from the storage spaces around the vehicle.

It didn't matter. They were safe.

The Bleeding Man was outside, and they were inside. "Shut the door!" Vic shouted, giving the order this time.

Hank pulled back hard on the handle, so much so that he feared he'd turn the whole ambulance inside out, smashing himself and the EMTS into a bloody pulp along the way.

But when Vic's hand touched his shoulder and Hank realized he'd been standing there with the door closed, watching as the Bleeding Man stood and resumed the consumption of his scarlet-hued flesh bit by stringy, meaty bit, then and only then did Hank release his gentle grasp of the handle and step back from the doors.

Before he climbed into the driver's seat, Vic leaned to him, her hand over her mouth and his ear all in one motion. Her eyes darted to the still-seated Darren, then back to Hank. As if that glance were enough to confirm suspicions Hank already shared. "Was that a zombie?" she asked in a rumbling whisper.

Hank shook his head. Adamant. Definitive.

"Nah," he said, "Zombies don't eat themselves."

Chapter 8

Closing in on the Bay Bridge, to say there was a traffic jam to get out of the city was a bit of an understatement. Nothing like the chaos back the way they'd come though, Hank and company didn't spy any more angry, violent mobs running wild in the streets. No Bleeding Men or Women either. Like the crew of Ambulance 7, everyone still alive in this part of the city remained encased in their steel and glass, four-wheeled cocoons. Mostly compact cars and mid-sized pick-ups, the kind of small sensible vehicles you're meant to survive the apocalypse in. No big trucks, no buses. Nothing so easily devastated by the earthquake and its aftershocks.

The NPR woman hadn't mentioned anything about BART, no word if the trains were running underground or above. Hank couldn't imagine they were. When he tried to picture the train, he saw it smashed to pieces by tunnels shaken apart like a child's block tower. He saw the long silver cars flattened and firing sparks like blood droplets.

He imagined the earth beneath their tires, turning itself over to reveal a silver spear, a wound through its heart. The people, crushed inside the earth and on top of the earth, were all so many specks of dust.

This was the part of Hank's inevitable sleep-deprived daydream when Darren would interrupt. When he'd make some smart-ass comment or off-color joke or just shout Hank's name until he was hoarse. That was the arrangement with which they'd started their quest: Hank leading as conductor and Darren shoveling coal into the engine to keep them barreling forward.

But Darren was silent, and Hank found himself saddled with the hard work of swimming up through bleary, prophecy-thickened visions without a voice from the outside world to guide him. He shook his head, then took his hands off the wheel to slap the sides of his head. Once, twice, three times.

"Vic, you okay back there?" he asked, after opening his eyes to find the ambulance inches from tapping the bumper of a black town car.

She grunted her reply. Vic was no longer buckled and instead sat on the floor, her knees drawn up against her chest.

"D?" Hank figured he had to say something, had to try and re-establish the connection. After all, he was the one blacking out, getting lost in a maze of complex thoughts. He reasoned Darren might be going through something similar, having witnessed the same death and destruction.

So Hank counted it as a small victory when Darren answered him. "Sure," he said.

Ahead, the town car shuffled forward an inch or two. Then, the ambulance followed, filling the void where the town car's back tires had rested.

Then, another standstill.

The debris was too widespread along the sidewalk, cutting off any potential routes for circumventing the traffic they were stuck in. Hank squeezed the steering wheel and then released his grasp. Repeating the process over and over, psyching himself up.

He thought of his kids, waiting back at the apartment with their sitter. He hoped the babysitter hadn't left the kids before the quake hit. Even if it *was* past the time when Hank'd promised to be home and despite her warnings that she had to leave on time and not a minute later because of her roller derby. Or if she had left, then maybe, at least, she'd doubled back and offered some reassurances to Marcy and Abel. A promise she'd stay until their father made it home.

Not that the kids would act worried or upset. Sometimes, it was as though they'd given up too much of their raw, wounded, and vulnerable insides when their mother passed away. The days after Livia died, Hank felt like he was walking around with lemon juice-soaked hands covered in open wounds, causing mind-blowing pain with every attempted embrace or caress with the only two people left that he could bring himself to give a damn about.

"Fuck it," he whispered and reached over, flicking on the lights and siren. The ambulance's shrieking call ripped through the tentative calm of trembling engines around them. Red light splattered the wreckage. As though the earth was bleeding.

Hank revved the engine. "Hold on back there, Vic!"

She gripped the edge of the bench.

Then, Hank slammed a meaty paw against the steering wheel's horn and added a baleful cry to the siren's steady screaming.

The message being delivered was a simple one. Easy enough for even the most traumatized survivor to comprehend:

MOVE!

Lucky for the crew of Ambulance 7, their message was received, and the results were in their favor. Like budding branches extending from the trunk, the vehicles and their drivers moved to the side, leaving the roadway. They pulled up against rubble piles and other shattered remnants of city life. Hank accelerated, taking the place of the town car, then the next car and the next truck, on and on. Moving ever forward.

The drivers and passengers in the other vehicles didn't turn their heads to watch the passing ambulance. Muscle memory compelled them to make way for the emergency vehicle. After all, that was the thing you did when you heard the sirens and saw flashing lights. You moved to the side and waited until that specter of injury or death passed.

So, as the ambulance and its three-person crew leapfrogged ahead toward a viable exit from the city, the vehicles it passed joined, becoming the tail, stuck straight out from behind. As a result, the chain of cars and trucks resembled an animal sensing danger and going on high alert.

Inside Ambulance 7, the uncomfortable thoughts forcing their way out of Hank's head replaced the sounds of the siren and horn.

"Kentwood...Kentwood...Kendra!"

Hank's shout didn't snap Darren out of whatever stupor he was suffering through. But it did rouse Vic. "What's going on?" she asked.

Confident now that the other vehicles were moving and the path was clear, Hank risked a look to the rear of the ambulance. "Vic, your cell phone, I need it. You went out with my kids' babysitter, right?"

"Uh...."

"You did. After the Fourth of July barbecue."

The slow light of a revisited memory warmed the EMT's initially confused face. "Oh...yeah. She was a little older."

"Yeah, yes, exactly." Hank took a hand from the wheel and held it back to Vic. "Let me see your phone. I wanna call her, check in and see how the kids are doing."

Inside, he cursed himself for not remembering Vic's connection to the sitter earlier. As though he had any control over the way his mind worked when facing complete disaster.

As her hands moved to her pockets, Vic blushed. " I don't even know if I got her number. Or if I kept it..."

Hank wiggled his fingers in nervous anticipation. "I still have to try," he said.

The crash behind the ambulance offered a sudden, sharp shock to the systems of everyone inside the ambulance. Even Darren flinched in his seat. Vic had pulled her phone out, along with her flask. Both items fell and clattered against the floor. The metal flask against the padded flooring produced a hollow *thunk*.

The sirens spun and howled, washing the world around them in an anemic bloody red. "What the hell was that?" Hank asked, already checking the rearview.

He expected to find the caravan of vehicles stretching into the infinite behind them. But the line of waiting traffic was smaller somehow.

Then another crash, followed by an explosion. Screams. Nightmare sounds ping-ponged across the remaining cars until reaching the ears of the crew from Ambulance 7.

Vic crawled and put her face up to one of the small, square windows on the ambulance's backdoors. She gazed out and back the way they'd come, even as Hank steered them around the remaining vehicles still ahead.

The sounds bouncing off the ruins of the city Hank had worked in for years weren't the sounds of disaster. These were no aftershocks, no crumbling structures giving up the ghost at last. No, these sounds reminded Hank of his time in the desert. They reminded him of getting stuck an ambush at a sketchy checkpoint. Heavy artillery fire from weapons donated by the good ol' U.S. of A to help stem the tide of dirty commies turned instead to the purpose of forestalling America's project of encroachment.

One glance wouldn't hurt though, right? One quick look meant Hank could understand what had Vic sobbing. Her face remained pressed to the window glass, even as cries racked her body.

After he looked, Hank sure as hell wished he hadn't.

Chapter 9

Tentacles.

Of all the things Hank might've guessed were causing the disturbance behind them, he wouldn't have ever landed on tentacles.

No matter how many chances he was given.

The slimy, sticky undersides of the massive wriggling cephalopodic limbs were everywhere all at once, bursting from sinkholes where buildings stood hours before. They filled the receding horizon like a drug-induced hallucination. One, two, three, eight, nine, ten...hundreds. Thick as oxen. Long as city blocks, maybe longer. Those standing vertically resembled the wacky inflatable figures set up outside used car dealerships. Waving in the desperate and gullible for a chance at a bargain.

One tentacle wrapped around a car three or four lengths back from the ambulance. It flexed, crushing metal and glass like tissue paper. Then, it withdrew from sight, back into the earth, taking the tiny Toyota Tercel and its unfortunate occupants with it.

Another equally monstrous appendage flopped down to take the place of the one before. It smacked the ground alongside an untold number of its counterparts, lewd and obscene in their blind pursuit of contact with something solid. Breaking more asphalt, crushing black rock into a cloud of dust that covered the sky in shadow like volcanic ash. Hank couldn't tell what the army of tentacles was even attached to. And he didn't want to know the answer either.

Working in unison, the phalanx of tentacles destroyed the vehicles behind the ambulance and ripped up the road as well. But even as the earth was torn open from underground, no single source for the wriggling, curling, slapping, slashing limbs revealed itself. Only more tentacles. Tentacles on top of tentacles. A mass congregation of sucker-dotted appendages, twisting and twirling around each other. Like fornicating worms.

Like snakes. Like a den of snakes when you lift a rock and expose their cool bellies to the scorching heat of the desert sun.

"You'd better drive."

Darren's comment caught Hank by surprise. But only because he'd been so quiet up until then. His point was a good one though. Hank slammed his foot down on the accelerator. He moved the steering wheel, all herky-jerky. It was as if he was watching his life on a screen, sped up, going faster and faster with each interval. Like the decisions he made—to *turn left, right, watch out, go straight, now right*—were not his own, but a recording played back seconds after the events happened.

Vic crawled from the back, heading toward the front seats. Her eyes were red. Her cheeks scratched as though she'd raked her fingernails down as penance for having seen the terror approaching.

Hank swerved when the black town car was tossed like crushed beer can over the ambulance. The car hit with an explosive crack, like firework poppers. A tiny puff of smoke in the overall maelstrom of chaos.

The ambulance tilted to the right, hard. Both tires on Hank's side came off the shattered roadway.

When they came down, Hank bit his tongue. The warm, wet taste of blood filled his mouth. He spat without thinking, spritzing cherry red mist against the windshield.

The noise from the attacking tentacles grew louder, amplified a thousand-fold. This time, Hank didn't have to look back to understand why. He didn't need to pick up on the fact that Vic's cries were becoming more obscured, muffled within the cacophonic symphony of destruction.

He understood what'd happened.

He knew the writhing mass of monstrous tentacles rising from the ground below had torn away the ambulance doors. Like they were picking scabs off a scraped knee.

Vic, I'm sorry.

Hank didn't say the words. He merely thought them. And he hoped they were enough of a comfort for wherever Vic was headed.

She could say nothing in reply anyway. Her mouth, chest, and the entirety of her being were wrapped up by dueling tentacles. They gripped her tight, before lifting her off the floor. As Hank, at the wheel of the ambulance, drove forward, the tentacles held Vic, ceasing their own forward progression.

They ripped her from the back of the ambulance as a result. His face hot and wet, Hank reached across and slapped Darren's chest, striking him hard as he could. Trying to pull him back to reality. "What's happening back there?" he screamed, "Tell me what's happening!"

Hank's hand stung, the pain traveling from his palm up to his shoulder; but the blow had its desired effect. Darren turned to the back, staring wide-eyed into the swirling mass of tentacles. The bulbous limbs engorged with slime held Vic somewhere in their depths.

"They have Vic," Darren said, stating the obvious with a voice devoid of emotion.

This time, Hank let his partner's stiffness pass by unremarked upon. After all, what emotions could contain the enormity of what they were witnessing? They faced something worse than crumbling buildings or shifting tectonic plates or untold numbers of dead even. They drove on, fleeing a world of make-believe terrors brought to life.

"They're pulling her into one of their holes. They're pulling everyone down."

Hank wanted to believe he was leaving the nightmare behind.

But he was a soldier deep in his heart. That would never leave him. He understood you never left the nightmare. You only struggled to find new ways to carry on inside it.

The ambulance hit a bump, and, as they came down, Hank glanced to the back once again. Vic's cell phone, damp with tentacle slime, slid across the floor.

And there it was, Hank's little ray of sunshine in the dark.

Chapter 10

As they approached the overpass, Darren counted the nude figures lined up along the railing. Hank kept his eyes on the road. That churning feeling in his gut, the one he used to get back in the desert when he *knew* things were about to go to shit had come back with the vengeance of decades.

"Twenty-three...twenty-four...goddamn, Hank. There are twenty-five people up there."

Somehow, with Vic gone...wherever she'd been taken to, a little bit of the old Darren returned. Hank was grateful for it. Having some black humor helped make the nightmare a bit more tolerable, even if it didn't erase the pain.

The nude, knock-kneed assemblage, waiting on the crumbling overpass with their mouths open and Adam's apples bobbing, chests heaving, droned on in atonal harmonies that barely penetrated the vehicles passing below their perch. The nude chorus served as an embodiment of the demented dreamscape in which the remaining members of Ambulance 7 journeyed.

The road ahead was slick and shiny, enough for a casual observer to mistake it for brand-new. Or to think a rainstorm had passed through, just ahead of the ambulance. But Hank knew better. The skies weren't black with storm clouds, but with smoke, those last gasped breaths from all the structures obliterated on the San Francisco side of the Bay.

There was no telling what poisons had been unleashed into the air. Hank hated that the back doors were open, exposing them to whatever ill wind circulated across the crippled roadways. He could only imagine what he and Darren were breathing in or absorbing into their bloodstreams with each passing moment. He went back to the burn pits overseas. Military equipment and recovered Taliban spoils set ablaze to keep them from enemy hands. Never mind what this burning will do to those who stood near the pits, stoking those flames. There wasn't time to ask questions or complain when playing the part of an American hero after all.

Except this wasn't overseas. This was home.

Or close to it. *So damn close.*

A fiery blue electrical spark sliced across the sky above the ambulance. Not lightning though. It moved parallel to the ground. A power surge of neon, a fiery comet shining in contrast to the gray, black, and brown ruins of the city. The light reflected off the slick road ahead, revealing a deep red saturated into the damp surface.

The same red splattered across the back of the ambulance.

The cracked cement posts holding up the overpass were like the slumping shoulders of a collapsing drunkard. *Could they make it under the overpass without the whole thing coming down on top of them?*

That was the million-dollar question.

The ambulance's arrival at the site was imminent, and with it would come the answers.

"I think they're gonna jump," Darren whispered.

At least, that's what Hank thought he heard above the ringing in his ears. Above the surging roar of the engine as he compressed the gas all the way to the floor. Above the primal scream released from deep in his belly, deep down where his worry and fear and panic swirled, hardening themselves into a diamond of discontent.

Hank drove on. At one point, a loud *pop* sounded, and the ambulance jerked to the left. Hank drove into the skid, then forced the wounded vehicle back to the middle of the lane.

Next, the *rain* fell. Like sheets of heavy precipitation dropping to the road behind them. *Fump fump fump fump*...on and on. A steady metronomic beat. Like beating drums and chanting voices.

Ahead, darkness stretched and pled to be held, ready to wrap Hanks's head in its oily embrace. Exploding stars, supernovas signaling the imminent death of far-off celestial bodies, went off like fireworks. But before they could provide any illumination, they faded away to blue lines, like the tracers Hank saw when he took mushrooms that one time out in the desert with some of the last buddies he'd kept from the war.

Hank wanted to nothing more than to drive into the abyss. At that moment, he believed there was no other choice left for them. But that changed when he felt Darren's hand on his shoulder.

"Open your eyes, Hank."

Chapter 11

The rain Hank heard driving under the overpass with his eyes shut tight had seemingly passed within his brief period of self-inflicted blindness. The asphalt ahead was dry. Everything *was* dry. Of course, the wreckage remained covered in a film of dust and ash courtesy of the massive earthquake and its many aftershocks. Seeing that powdered devastation made one thing clear: it was not rain that Hank heard before.

He recalled the naked wriggling figures chanting and gyrating as they stood in formation past the overpass's safety railing.

"Did they *really* jump?" he asked.

The way Darren didn't respond was answer enough.

Not wanting to ask follow-up questions, Hank took this latest bit of tragedy and shoved it down inside. Not so much to compartmentalize it, as to sweep it under a rug, where it might get lost—one dark thought among many.

At the very least, Hank appreciated that Darren had stopped trying to get him to pull over the ambulance and help any more of the injured or distraught they passed. After the Bleeding Man and what happened to Vic, it wasn't something the driver was willing to entertain, even if his partner tried to make the case once more.

As if thinking about her was an invocation, Vic's cell phone rattled in the back of the vehicle. Hank took a glance to make sure it was still near at hand. *Miracle of miracles*, it was, though it did sit closer to Darren's seat than Hank's. With his right elbow, the driver nudged the EMT across the center console.

"Vic's cell," Hank said, "Can you grab it?"

Darren reached for the phone. His chest pressed against the restraining seatbelt. Fingertips came close to the rectangular phone case, and yet...he came up short.

He unclicked his seatbelt. This time, Hank didn't slow down or stop. Instead, he drove at a steady clip. Even as the busted driver's side tire beat its deflated vulcanized rubber across the road's gritty surface, Hank refused to cede ground to the laws of nature. He'd keep the ambulance moving until not a single hubcap remained as far as he was concerned.

Darren stretched to the back, hanging half of his body across the center console. Hank was half-convinced Darren would slither to the back, body wriggling like one of the tentacles they'd left behind.

Left behind with Vic.

But before his imagination ran away with that vision of Darren devolved into some limb of a prehistoric cephalopod, the EMT returned to his seat and showed off Vic's phone with something close enough to the old Darren's grin.

"Got it!" he said.

"Look for a Kendra...uh I don't remember her last name though."

Darren studied the green glow of Vic's phone screen. His thumb slid across the smeared glass. "Got a lot of names in here. A lot of K names for that matter!"

"Lot of sailors," Hank said.

It was an old joke shared between the trio. *Another one at Vic's expense.* Before she was gone, Hank hadn't noticed how that was the case with so many of their inside jokes. As though Darren (and Hank as well) knew which of their number was the weakest and made sure to punish her in kind. As a result of this lingering guilt, Hank worried he'd done wrong when the words left his mouth. He feared Darren might clam up and revert to the strange behavior he'd displayed earlier. So, it was a welcome surprise when a chuckle came from the passenger seat.

Darren's laughter grew to a belly-shaking guffaw and Hank joined in. Tears roll fat and salty from his eyes. They served double duty, the resulting product of their shared delirious mirth and as a form of mourning.

"I ever tell you the worst call I ever went on?" Darren asked. "Before you, I mean?"

There was an awkward pause. Then, he continued, "I mean before all *this* obviously."

Hank hesitated, uncertain how to respond. But when Darren continued running his finger across Vic's screen to scroll for the babysitter's info, he figured it was okay to proceed. "No. I don't think ya did, D."

It was the truth. Hank found most of the EMTs never wanted to share too much about past calls. It was a feeling he could identify with. After all, he had more than enough tales of his own, shaped under the merciless sun, that he'd vow to keep until his dying days. He understood that some burdens were meant to be carried alone.

"We got a call...Vic, me, and our old driver Eddie. She and Vic were dating at the time. Used to confuse the hell out of folks when I told 'em I had dating co-workers named Eddie and Vic.

"Anyway, the call was about this warehouse blaze...one of those artists' spaces they've got on both sides of the Bay. Partly a homeless squat, but with Basquiat street art flair, if ya get my drift? Kind of place where the smell of incense and patchouli has only a slight edge over the stench of stale shit..

"Our job's to be one of several ambulances on the scene to take any survivors the fire crew manages to extract from the building. But the way that place's going up like campfire kindling, we're not expecting to be particularly busy.

"You know how easy it is to get lost staring into the yellow part of the flames, right? The glimmer takes hold and makes your eyes water but also forces ya to keep 'em open? It was that exact thing. Just the three of us watching the fire...

"Until I noticed the woman covered by a black blanket, gripping the silver-handled cooking pot tight in tremoring hands.

"I got Vic and Eddie's attention. All three of us hopped out. It was one of those all-hands-on-deck-in-seconds types of situations. Because once I got a better look at the woman draped in her blanket, it became damn clear the cotton-like threads I'd watched come free from the covering with every stumbling step, weren't from a *blanket* at all. It was ash, char. The woman was burnt to a damn crisp.

"She stumbled even more when we got closer. I remember Vic exhaling like she'd been holding her breath the whole time waiting for this ash-coated figure to reach us. And the black covering over the woman's flesh blew away with just a breath, leaving her as this open wound of a person. All white and pink. Flesh and bone exposed to the elements. I don't even know how she made it out of the fire. I dunno how she made it as far as she did.

"Her eyes melted, dribbling down her cheeks. And her hands were fused to the pot, ruined skin bubbling around the silver handles.

"Vic and Eddie threw up. And I was damned close myself. But then, the woman spoke to me. *To us.* Her voice... I'll never forget it. Not a trace of irritation, none of that smoke-filled wheeze you'd expect given the circumstances she'd emerged from. Instead, it was the sweetest whisper. Like a child's. 'Is my baby warm now?' she asked.

"The lid slid off her pot. And I looked inside. Damn me, I looked."

Chapter 12

Silence joined them, a new passenger in the ambulance. Hank couldn't tolerate its presence.

Chapter 13

Hank's hands worked the steering wheel as if it owed him gambling debts. Squeezing tight, easing up for a better grip, and then doing it all over again. Finally, he started talking.

Darren didn't interrupt him.

"Before they assigned me to drive with you and Vic, they sent me on a few training rounds. Ride-alongs, right? Wanted me to see how the ambulance handled, to get used to people getting the fuck out of your way once you turned the red lights on and let the sirens rip.

"Like I wasn't already used to that from my time in Kabul. Like I hadn't been behind the controls of an actual fucking death machine...

"But whatever. I figured I needed the job. I mean...I *didn't*. I'd left the army with a nice pension, having put in my time in some of the most hellish places on Earth. I could've taken some time off. Gone back to college. Could've really been all that I could be.

"Except Livia went and walked into our kitchen from the tiny bathroom holding that test with those two blue lines on it. She was crying, and everything changed.

First, there was Marcy, and she was our everything. But not for long enough though. Livia had to go back to work pretty soon after Marce was born.

"I didn't even think anything of it when the woman I love cried again after we had sex on our anniversary. Call it women's intuition, but she seemed to know far more about what the future held for us. I came inside her and then Marce woke up in the converted nursery space in the living room, screaming her lungs out for all the world to hear. Like she thought we might've forgotten about her.

"Her head on the pillow, the perfect midnight of Livia's skin glistened with tears. I thought she was happy. I thought she was glad I was coming home to stay because that's how *I* felt about it. I put my shit onto her like she was nothing more than a reflection of my dreams, my hopes, and my desires. Then, I rolled over and went to sleep, leaving her to put Marcy back to bed.

"The second test with the blue lines showed up and brought more tears. At least, I recognized there was a problem that time. Too little, too late, all things considered. But the shrink I saw a couple of times after Liv...guy told me I needed to find ways to ease my burden. You know, for the kids? 'You don't want them to feel like they're losing you as well,' he'd say.

"Of course, I put finding the solution to Livia's problems onto myself. Mister Real American Hero coming to save the day, you understand? That pushed me to start driving the ambulance. Signed up after we brought Abel home.

"Now that we're caught up, let's go back to the ride-alongs. This one night in particular they had me working in Oakland, so I'd be close to Livia and the kids. I remember it clearly, how I was sitting in the front passenger seat like you're doing now.

"Fairly uneventful night as far as they go. We'd just given this sweet old abuela who'd broken her hip a ride to the hospital and then a call came in from the dispatcher...

"I knew, *okay*? Even though I didn't say anything at the time when they gave us the address, even though I rode with the crew in silence while they cracked jokes and shot the proverbial shit. I *knew*.

"Ambulance requested. Gunshot wound. Self-inflicted. Two minors present.

"I fucking knew the whole time.

"Livia didn't shoot herself in the head with my service revolver. Nothing like that. She did it in her heart, leaving a ruined bloom coming through the sheet they pulled over her body. I learned that later. Someone felt bad for me, as I was crying, making blubbery, slobbery threats that no one took seriously, and they filled me in.

"I missed it the first time around because I didn't wait in the vehicle like they told me and ran up the stairs screaming Livia's name the whole way instead. It took one of the EMTs and a couple of neighbors to hold me down. Cops on the scene had to taze me a few times and later some of 'em said they were worried they'd have to shoot me. They were making jokes about the *trouble they'd* get into. Fuckin' pigs.

"Why didn't you?" I remember asking them. Of course, it's less of a memory and more like a clip from a movie trailer, showing a piece of the whole but never the entire picture.

"I didn't kill anyone that night either. Everyone lucked out on that count..."

"And the kids?" Darren's voice is soft, weighed down with an understanding of what the answer will be.

The nearest car was several miles ahead of them, but they were gaining on it fast. Fast, fast, faster. Until Hank let up on the gas, just shy of bumping into the sagging chrome bumper before them. Everything smelled like burning. The busted tires—there were at least two of them on the ambulance, the road itself, the air. Somehow *everything* was on fire.

The ambulance driver's throat felt like was a fire-eater, downing spinning balls of flame, as he finally choked out an answer.

"First responders found them. Marcy holding Abel. Both of them dipping their fingers in the ruined place where their mother's heart should've been."

Darren offered nothing in return for Hank bearing his soul. A red-hot flush of anger coursed through Hank's body, and he squeezed the steering wheel tight. In doing so, he clipped the release button on the steering column, sending the wheel plunging to the floor. His stomach dropped with it and his foot slipped over to the brake.

Somehow, he missed Darren taking off his seatbelt again. But he didn't miss the skinny EMT slamming hard against the console in response to the sudden stop. Hank winced at the cracking sound made by Darren's breaking ribs. He waited to see Darren turn with bruised and jaundiced skin around his eyes, lenses heavy with a cloud of tears.

But nothing like that happened.

Instead, Darren took crooked hands, with one bent-back finger on each, and pushed himself off the console. He left his seat and bound to the back.

Hank shrugged. After all, there was only so much strangeness a man could encounter in a life-or-death situation like they'd found themselves in, before any brief flashes of the weird faded to background noise.

"Gonna try the radio again," Hank said.

When Hank gave the dial a fresh spin, he found more static than on his previous attempts. Building white noise like menacing tides threatening to swallow a seashore whole and take everything with it. A roaring hiss meant to leave a listener tired, hungry, and disoriented. Hank pictured the ambulance as a life raft, set adrift in the middle of the Pacific—with a cruel sun poking and prodding them under a cloudless sky.

Finally, his sweaty, twitchy fingers slipped on the dial and Hank found himself back on the local NPR station. Whatever fate had befallen the newsreader, it was clear she'd taken her talent for dry monotone readings of the day's host of horrors and gone elsewhere.

At first, there was nothing there. *Only silence.* At least, it wasn't static though. Hank took small comfort in that fact. The streets were tightly-packed along the route to the bridge. Which made sense given how many people likely had the same idea as him. He took the fact that the road ahead wasn't more debris-strewn or littered with abandoned vehicles and broken, bloody bodies as a positive omen. He let himself believe it showed his hypothetical *others* were able to get through and leave the city. He imagined them all over in the East Bay, reunited with their loved ones.

Hank needed to believe because he wished that same fate for himself.

But before he'd driven father, a thrum, like some ancient organ with all its keys pressed at once emanated from the radio, interrupting Hank's reverie. The chanting followed almost immediately. Deep, throaty rumblings that sounded as though an entire choir sang from deep down in a well or a mineshaft, their basso profundo voices echoing off slime-slick stones, dirt, and animal bones. The voices climbed from the depths, until they blended into one. No single member of this choir of the damned ever overtaking the other.

Hank's stomach rumbled. Hunger overtook him. Not just the physical kind, but a spiritual longing as well. His ears filled with chanting. His skull rattled inside the too-thin layer of flesh around it. The song, such as it was, reminded him of the noise he'd heard faintly from the nude, wriggling forms on the overpass, those cultists waiting to plummet to the earth below. Somewhere in the toneless, wordless—or at least no words *he knew*—evocations, Hank thought there might be an answer to find. But he wasn't so certain he wished to hear it.

The clear path ahead Hank noted moments before was taken away from him. The buildings left standing, those in crumpled like God's bad drafts tossed into the waste, the road in segments smooth and jagged, all the pieces of reality were twisted and turned in on themselves. This vision resembled a kaleidoscope in the hands of an overeager child forever rotating the toy, making the pictures shatter, then rebuild into stranger geometric formations. Close to the original image, but never the same. Then, moving farther and farther away from the truth with every turn.

Hank's knuckles were ashen white, like gravestones bumping through the dark brown on the backsides of his hands. Fighting against every instinct to stop, to give in and go mad, he kept driving forward.

His mouth was dry, parched. Faster and faster, the landscape flipped and flopped. A dying fish snatched from the water and left to choke on oxygen.

Still refusing to fall victim to the madness infecting the rest of reality, Hank closed his eyes. He would deny the world laid out before him.

After all, the path ahead as seen through dried-out, exhausted orbs in his head wasn't reliable any longer. Instead, he'd focus on the vision in his head, Marcy and Abel—the only ones left who truly mattered to him. Thinking only of them would provide him with the best path forward. Or so he believed.

Darren's arms shot forward from the back of the vehicle. Reaching from behind the driver's seat, the EMT held Hank fast against the seat with one hand, and with the other, he pressed the razor-sharp blade of a scalpel to the big man's neck.

Hank's eyes opened, taking in the bloody sight of Darren's fingers. Each digit was relieved of the thick keratin covering of his nails, replaced with oozing wounds that left sloppy trails of sticky wetness down the driver's neck.

Unable to speak, unable to pray, Hank could only act. He cranked the steering wheel hard as he could, steering to the right, steering into the scalpel-holding hand of the man who looked like Darren.

But he wasn't any Darren that Hank knew. Not anymore.

Chapter 14

There's a moment in every blockbuster action or disaster-run-amuck flick, where the protagonist's behind the wheel of a fast-moving vehicle and loses control for a split second. Then, Steve McQueen or Bruce Willis or The Rock goes careening off the road and their stunt driver slams into some prop. A newsstand. A garbage can. Maybe some traffic cones and a roadblock sawhorse on a parade route. Always something that makes for a nice impact on-screen, but that never results in the death of the hero-driver or whatever poor saps might be on the road with them at the same time. In Hank's case, as he lost control of the ambulance and drove into the skid, it was a fire hydrant that served as his collision point.

The right side of the rescue vehicle hit the yellow-painted hydrant hard, crumpling the passenger side. Hank was grateful to still have his seatbelt strapped across his bulk, as the left-hand tires rose off the broken road and the axles groaned.

Darren wasn't so lucky. He slipped and fell, then slid across the back of the ambulance. When he hit the crumpling wall, his hand opened, dropping the scalpel. His breath whistled between his teeth and a grin spread across his face like a disease.

As the left-hand side of the vehicle gave into gravity and returned to the earth, Hank wiped at the thin trickle of blood on his neck, oozing where he'd been nicked. He winced.

Partly from the pain, certainly. But also from the knowledge of how much worse it could've been. He understood that the surprise of the initial ambush was just the first part of the danger. His thumb pressed down on the seatbelt release, and he launched himself into the back, his fist leading the way. His knuckles slammed through cartilage and drove down to the bone of Darren's nasal plate.

The crunch and spray of blood were made worse by the demonic grin plastered onto the lower half of the EMT's face. Even as blood and bone shards dribbled like chunky peanut butter past his lips, Darren kept smiling and whispering with a sing-song intonation, his indecipherable speech matching the deeper chanting coming from the radio.

Using the driver's seat and passenger's seat for support, just like Darren had done what seemed like a lifetime ago, Hank kicked out, letting the soles of his boots get up close and personal with Darren's chest, pushing the other man backward.

The scalpel was in Darren's hand again. Even befouled with blood, broken physically and mentally, he kept a firm hold on the bladed instrument. He swung his arms in wide, sweeping, slicing arcs. Laughing, *always laughing*.

Hank dodged the silvered edges of the scalpel. Ducking and weaving like he'd found himself in a boxing match with Freddy Krueger. He knew what he needed to do. He was bigger and stronger than his friend. It should've been a simple enough task to land some heavy blows and finish things.

But this wasn't a day for simple tasks. For every five or six times, Hank dodged the blade, Darren would land a stinging strike with another. Hank's skin opened along his arm, splitting like parted lips. Switching to a different tack, he put his head down and charged at Darren like a bull.

The top of his head collided with an instrument pan, denting the shiny metal. Following his "shield" maneuver, Darren swung his trusty "sword," bringing the scalpel down full force at the side of Hank's head. Once again like a bull, Hank bellowed in rage and pain. The former silence he'd found so welcoming was now gone, replaced by the chanting and by the spray of blood as it flowed down the side of his head from the spot where his ear dangled.

The pain came like a wall of heat, and Hank's eyelids fluttered in response. He yelled again, pulling deep from some reservoir of strength, some source left untapped even through war and Livia's death.

Hank's blood fountained and ricocheted off the walls of the ambulance hitting him in his eye. Hot tears mixed with hot blood and his ears rang.

"Hank..."

His name came through muffled, distorted. Half-blind and searching, Hank's breaths came in jagged bursts. Darren waited at the back of the ambulance, facing his friend and co-worker.

Darren's features had returned to some semblance of *normal*. A great sadness etched across his face, even as he gave Hank a look that managed to suggest hope—for them, for the future, for the world.

But it was too little, too late. Hank's hands were already on the wheeled gurney. Giving it a hard kick with his boot, he unlocked it from its docking position. Once freed, it flew toward the open back-door of the ambulance.

Thinking back on the split-second between the push and the gurney's impact with Darren's mid-section, Hank would swear he saw the twisted devil's grin returning to the EMT's face. He'd embrace that memory, whether real or wished-for, because it was the only path that allowed him to continue.

They'd made it so far. The crew of Ambulance 7.

Darren had almost made it to the bridge. The signs directing traffic that way were all around them.

But Darren's time in the ambulance had reached its end. Not with an explosion or an evisceration, nothing like that. When the gurney hit him, he lost his balance and fell backward. He didn't scream or shout or gasp. He simply fell.

The *snap* of his neck on broken concrete marking the end of his descent and of his life was a small, insignificant thing. Like the front door creaking open in a house you're certain is haunted after you step on the lawn, and so you run away red-faced, panting, laughing.

Hank stared down at his dead friend. Darren had always been smaller than Hank. But there on the ground, he was a shattered doll of a man. A porcelain figurine smashed, as though God were some negligent collector, bumping into their display case.

Even for all the words that Hank may have wanted to say, the eulogies he could've delivered, the shrill shrieking of pain was such that the time and opportunity to lament what was lost became too much to ask for. Instead, he ransacked the supplies in the ambulance until he found white medical tape and gauze. He bound his ear tight to his blood-slicked head, though it only served to capture the throbbing of the blood and gore oozing from his wound. Like he'd held up a seashell from hell and could hear the fiery pits lapping against the jagged stones of the eternal abyss.

He returned to the driver's seat. When he was halfway there, he took one more look behind him. At first, Hank thought he was doing it for Darren. But then he noticed the slim black rectangle of Vic's phone. Even with the doors ripped off, the ambulance nearly flipped, and both Vic and Darren dead, his silly little phone had somehow lived on.

Hank scooped it up. Once he was in the driver's seat, he gave the device a quick inspection. The screen glass was smashed, spiderweb patterns popping up across the green and black. But there was a glow under those surface wounds, and when Hank squinted he could make out the babysitter's name on the screen. "Kendra."

A loud rumble shook the earth. Hank tensed. Preparing for another round of aftershocks. But at the same time, he was unable and unwilling to wait for them to strike. Whatever proper procedure might dictate, Hank was far beyond caring. He turned the engine back on. No sputtering, no hesitation came from under the hood. The vehicle growled with as much determination to see their journey through to the end as consumed the man behind the steering wheel.

The noise below the earth grew louder and louder, vibrating until it felt as though Hank might drive on a road of trampolines. The shifting plates raced to an inevitable rendezvous, locked onto the ambulance's position. As Hank's foot pressed the accelerator to the floor, a fount of gray and black and brown sprayed up behind the vehicle. Along with the debris, more tentacles shot out from deep in the darkness. Everything from the monstrously huge limbs they'd encountered previously to thinner, spaghetti-like strands wriggling and writhing like baby snakes.

Again, the seemingly source-less limbs slapped and crashed on the pitted surface of the earth, blind, overeager beasts searching and searching.

Still determined to put as much distance between himself and those gooey, slime-drenched feelers, Hank hazarded a glimpse to the back. It was a choice he immediately regretted.

The tentacles held Darren's corpse in a standing position. Some wrapped around his broken neck, and others squeezed his midsection, so he appeared to bob like a buoy on the ocean. Still more tentacles held his legs, swinging them just above the rubble. A final set held his arms up. In this way, the dead man came to resemble some nightmare marionette.

The tentacles bent one of Darren's arms into a crook and then wagged his wrist. Back and forth, up and down.

Like they were making their puppet wave goodbye.

Chapter 15

This time, Hank didn't find it as easy to avoid the tentacles. As fast as he drove, as much ground as he covered, they always managed to pop up somewhere close behind, breaking through the earth and sending asphalt, concrete, and the heavy steel of manhole covers up into the sky. Like deadly confetti.

The explosive nature of the tentacles' efforts made for a hell of a celebration as Hank made it to the Bay Bridge. The wind howled, blowing dark clouds of poisoned smoke across the entrance. Peering through the windshield, Hank spotted these rolling balls of orange flame, dancing across the metal. They pulsed with heat. There appeared to be a steady flow to the traffic, even though the nearest car was so far ahead Hank couldn't make out much more than the indistinct blob of its shape through the noxious smog.

Preparing to merge into the single lane left open leading onto the bridge, Hank felt a sudden, sharp tug coming from the rear of the ambulance. He pressed down on the gas, letting the tires (or what remained of them) spin.

When he looked back, Hank had his worst fears confirmed. A new tentacled mass had its many-limbed grasp on the ambulance. He feared whatever entity controlled the slithering horde had its sights on a complete set of all three members of Ambulance 7.

Even as the wheels scrambled for purchase across the remnants of the road, the limbs held firm. They weren't quite pulling back on the bumper, not yet at the least, but they did hold it in place.

Hank pounded his fists against the steering wheel. In doing so, he activated its horn. Its loud, baleful cry was unleashed into the night. In making such a noise, the ambulance became a whale beached at low tide and unable to return to its loved ones still swimming past the breakers.

Vic's cell rested on top of the radio unit. Its light was faint but showed the device still worked. Hank had managed to turn it onto speakerphone, so even as the wheel wells were crunched under the tentacles' ministrations, he could pick out a faint ringing sound emanating from the device. Over and over, it went *brrrrrrng brrrrrrng brrrrrrng*. Hank had no intention of cutting the ringing short. He figured as long as it kept ringing, then there was a chance.

A chance someone was still there. A chance someone would pick up from the other side and he'd talk to his kids again.

Again, he'd tell them not to worry because Daddy would be home soon.

Just to get that chance was all the motivation he needed to ensure it's fulfillment. No matter what. Damn all the obstacles.

When the slimmer, worm-like tendrils branching from their more gargantuan brethren penetrated the ambulance's interior, they made a bee-line for the ringing, buzzing cell phone. As he ran the gas pedal hard and tried to free his vehicle from the tentacles' grasp, Hank noted how the smaller limbs flung themselves toward the phone—his final lifeline. There was an intelligence behind their actions.

Hank moved fast. With a savagery that would've brought forth tears and frightened screams from his children, if they'd seen him at the moment, his right hand left the steering wheel and squeezed a mass of the miniature tentacles. He pulled hard as if he could rip them free from whatever inconceivable source they originated from.

Quickly understanding the impossibility of his task, Hank opted for another approach. He pulled again, harder this time. He stretched the waving feelers to his lips, then past them. He brought his teeth down, squishing and grinding incisors, canines, and molars, to tear through the slime-slick skin of the tentacles.

His mouth soon filled with something like blood. But grittier, tasting like stone and sand, gravel. When it leaked out and ran down his chin, it was black. He spat. Gagged. Spat again, harder.

Darkness rushed past his lips and hit the radio. Sparks flew at the point of impact. The plastic casing melted. The tiny, wounded limbs fell from Hank's mouth. They were left limp, unmoving. Marking a victory—of sorts.

Teeth blackened by the blood, Hank smiled. "Got you..." He spat again. "Got you, bastards."

If those skinny, rat-tail-sized tentacles were the bastards, then their beefier, heftier purebred tentacle siblings would prove an even worthier foe. They worked as a unit, finally wrenching backward, dragging the bent and ruined wheels from the back of the ambulance and across the asphalt.

With his foot pressing the gas, Hank let the wheels spin and spin. The resulting friction cut through some of the tentacles, and Hank twisted the steering wheel back and forth to change the angles of attack. Left, right, and back again. Pus and gritty, grimy black blood flowed from the appendages. For every limb Hank severed, three more reared up from the ground and took on the task of assaulting the ambulance and pulling it backward.

Again, Hank screamed. Letting his voice get completely shredded. He punched the radio panel, jolting the phone. It flew up, then clattered down. But that wasn't what held his attention. Instead, his eyes were drawn to an A/C vent positioned near the radio. That particular vent hadn't worked for nearly as long as Hank had been driving Ambulance 7. However, repairs for the fleet were so backed up at the hospital, the message had always been "You're gonna have to wait and deal with it."

The vent parts were twisted and cracked from the impact of his fist. He used his fingers to pull away the shattered plastic. The unit popped out with a gasp. Hank's index finger and thumb snaked into the hole and closed around several *somethings*.

He returned his hand to the ambulance's interior light, revealing several minis of Belvedere vodka in his grasp.

He'd suspected Vic was stashing booze somewhere else aside from her flask. And here, he had his suspicions confirmed.

Poor Vic.

But maybe lucky me.

As he unscrewed the tops of the bottles, the heavy antiseptic scent of the heavily-proofed booze hit his nose. A plan formed almost instantly, something learned from his days in the war. Fighting insurgents, desperate men, women, and even children sometimes, many willing to do anything they could to hold onto their homes and their lives.

The one thing he'd learned as a result?

Everything was a weapon. *Everyone.*

He ripped at the bandage pressed to the side of his head until his fingernail tore away a nice strand, more or less free from the sticky oozing serum still flowing out of his wound. He ripped off more strands, until he had one per mini. He twisted them down into the bottles.

Then, he reached over to where the radio popped and sizzled from the contact with that viscous tentacle blood. Rather than dwell on what that same black liquid might be doing to his insides, Hank used the flames. He held the rags to the fire until they burned. The licking tongues raced up the cloth and back down into the glass, before reaching the combustible alcohol inside.

Waiting, waiting...until finally, he couldn't wait anymore—unless he wanted to have his hands blown off, Hank threw the miniature Molotov cocktails behind his head and into the writhing growth of tentacles.

A bellowed *whoosh* like a jet plane flying inches over top of the ambulance followed. Oxygen left Hank's lungs. Something wet splattered against the inside of the ambulance and hit the back of Hank's head. More tiny cuts opened on his neck and along the back of his head. Glass and bits of booze-covered tentacle wormed into his wounds.

But he was free.

The ambulance was free.

Hank drove onto the Bridge.

The smooth sound of wheels on the concrete of the bridge was drowned out almost entirely by the ringing in his damaged ears.

Almost, *but not quite*.

For all the ringing Hank heard, there was still one ringing he *didn't* hear.

The ringing of the cell phone.

Then, he heard a voice.

"Daddy...?"

Chapter 16

If asked to enumerate the tears shed as he listened to his son and daughter relay how they'd survived the earthquake Darren had dubbed "The Big One," Hank would've failed. There were simply too many to count. Hot and wet, they streamed forth, dampening his cheeks and soaking the collar of his shirt below his chin. Still, he let the kids—mostly Marcy, who was holding their babysitter's cell phone—talk and talk, sharing minute detail after minute detail.

"Ms. Kendra was getting ready to take us to the first floor to wait in the lobby. In the back corner, like you told us in our earthquake plan. Abel was taking a while because he wanted to bring his comic boo…"

"Nuh-uh! I already had my comic book. I wanted my juice cup."

Hank cleared his throat and silence followed on the other end of the line. He laughed, considering how funny it was to hear such a mundane argument play out between his children.

But when Marcy picked up her story, after shushing her brother one more time for good measure, Hank's laughter faded.

"We were on the stairs. Kendra went back to hurry Abel along. He ran through her legs, down to where I was. We were almost at the bottom, by the mailboxes. Then…"

Abel picked up the story baton and ran with it. "Daddy, the building fell down on us. All around us"

Again, Hank white-knuckled the steering wheel. Blood pumped at the side of his head, soaking the strips of cloth holding his ear in place. To say the words his children shared were hard to hear was an understatement.

"We woke up and it was so dusty. We were on the floor, but kind of under the floor. Like down in the dirt. We were close to the doors, so nothing hit us from the other apartments. Some glass fell inside...the crinkly ceiling fell too. It's hard to see where to go. But Kendra's cell phone landed down here next to us."

"That's good, baby," Hank said. "I'm glad you had her with you."

"No, Daddy. *She* didn't make it down the stairs Not all of her..."

A flood of images assaulted Hank's mind, envisioning the babysitter's hand or arm, grasping the cell phone—the sole lifeline to the crumbling world outside—before being severed by falling debris. He didn't ask his kids for more details.

"Well, I'm glad you have her phone. Glad you got my call."

"We heard it ringing and ringing. We're sorry it took so long to crawl over and answer, Daddy."

"Yeah!" Abel chimed in at the end.

Hank could hardly get the words out; his sobs were too rich to handle. "I'm on the bridge, okay? Daddy's coming home and we're all gonna be fine."

"Okay, Daddy. Bye-b..."

Before his daughter finished, Hank's panic got the better of him and he shouted, "No! Don't hang up that phone, Mabel Eileen! You stay on this line until Daddy's there, holding you in my arms. You understand?"

"Yes, Daddy." Their answers came in stereo.

\#

Hank drove on autopilot while he listened to his children. The initial flow of traffic on the bridge was smooth enough so he didn't have to pay too much attention. He maneuvered the ambulance like a Tetris piece, pinpointing the lane where he'd fit and then slotting himself into it.

His children mumbled over the phone. It didn't matter what they were saying. He just loved hearing their voices. The squeaks and chirps dimpling their hushed whispers were enough to give Hank the little extra boost of energy needed to see his journey through to the end. The sound of their tiny voices was enough to make him feel as though hope remained a possibility even when facing an apocalypse.

Checking the left lane to see if he might have room to speed up and bypass a car slightly ahead on that side, Hank glimpsed the driver peering over the wheel of her Jeep Cherokee. The SUV stood out on the road, given its hot-pink custom paint job and sorority tchotchkes hanging from the rearview mirror. But the driver, covered in a syrupy thick black tar that Hank soon understood was blood, looked as though she'd traveled through a Hell far worse than Jell-O shots and streaking in the quad.

Her eyes were visible, but they'd had all the color drained from them. They were white orbs, cobwebbed in cataracts.

She turned and her white, pupilless eyes met Hank's. An all-too-brief staring contest ensued.

Hank lost.

His foot slammed on the brake. The sudden friction against the bridge made sparks explode from under the ambulance. The steady flow of traffic had come to a stop. The ambulance fishtailed as Hank tried his damnedest to regain control. The tailgate knocked against several cars traveling in the right lane. They greeted him with screeching tires, honking horns, and drivers' epithets flung from open windows.

Hank had no desire to see what those drivers might look like.

More car horns honked like a gaggle of mad geese stirred to a fury. Before Hank joined the choir, he shoved open his driver's side door and craned his neck up, trying to spot the source of everyone's delay. He figured maybe there was some obstruction, a pair of cars T-boned across lanes. If so, he might venture forth, traveling on foot along the bridge's walking path, and help push the ruined cars aside, clearing a path to the other side for himself and the others.

That idea got thrown to the side and trampled, once the first man ran past the ambulance shrieking. Clad in t-shirt and board shorts with the piercings covering his face—each piece of metal glittering when struck by the light from the ambulance, the stranger's hair stood straight up and stiff, as though flash-frozen. Each follicle was as white as fresh-fallen snow.

It was only after the man sprinted past the ambulance that Hank noticed the trail of blood oozing across the bridge marking the man's attempted escape path.

Still leaning from the driver's side, Hank turned to follow the fleeing man. The runner didn't make it too far past the ambulance before collapsing. Hank could only stare in wide-eyed terror as more tentacles burst through the windshields of the many cars lined behind him. Some of the tentacles snaked along the surface of the bridge until they could grab the fallen man and pull him into their many-limbed embrace.

Even as the grotesque flopping of appendages echoed from behind the ambulance, Hank could pick out more tramping feet and shrieking voices coming from up ahead.

The trickle of one man turned into a crashing tidal wave of humanity.

Hank held his hand out as the next runner came, and when he felt cloth at his fingertips, he closed his fingers into a fist, bringing his catch to the ambulance. This time, the tears dampening his face were not his own. They belonged to another distraught bleeding white-haired runner.

"What's going on? What's happening up there?" Hank asked.

The man's lips, chapped, cracked, and oozing blood, formed words but it was hard to hear them over the banging and crashing, tentacles picking up cars and shaking loose morsels, then throwing the vehicles away like empty peanut shells in the bleachers at a baseball game.

Hank pulled the man even closer, letting the crying, wounded stranger's tears and blood baptize him anew. "What?" he asked again.

Despite his weakened, exhausted form, the man pushed away from Hank with an adrenaline-spiked burst of strength. In doing so, he managed to wriggle free. Just as he did, a pair of tentacles, thick as tractor tires, slammed against either side of his head. Before his skull got popped like a pimple though, he yelled his answer back to the ambulance driver.

"The Fish-Men! They're coming out of the Bay! They're..."

SPLAT!

Chapter 17

The kind of day Hank was having, wasn't the kind where he had the luxury of asking *What Fish-Men?*

He'd seen more than enough so that the words held no more absurdity for him than anything else he'd encountered. If the dead man, splattered across more abandoned cars in the lane beside the ambulance said Fish-Men existed, then that was true as far Hank was concerned. The only relevant response, nestling away as a tiny nugget in the back of his mind, was to consider whether or not he'd survive an encounter with these alleged Fish-Men and how he might do so.

His greater and more immediate worry came from his old friends the tentacles back for yet another round. Hank slammed the driver's side door closed and didn't bother buckling up again. He pressed the gas to the floor and the ambulance shot off like a battering ram. The Tesla in front of Hank's spot skipped across the bridge like he'd thrown a rock across a pond.

The sleek grey electric car transformed into a sleek grey electric car with flames bursting from its undercarriage and windows.

Hank swerved to avoid the flames and narrowly missed a cresting tentacle moving over the top of his vehicle's flashing red lights. The monstrous limb was roughly the size of a small aircraft. Its heftiness compared to the tentacles seen before was one more thing Hank had neither time nor inclination to wrestle with mentally.

"Daddy?"

There, on the phone, that was what Hank chose to focus on. His two kids, his whole world, waiting on the other side of the bridge.

"It's okay, babes," he said, using the nickname that they used to love but were already getting too big for and rolled their eyes at whenever he used it most days, "I'm coming home."

As if punctuation, the burning smart car exploded behind him and the fireball struck some of the pursuing tentacles, charring them to a crispy blackness.

That was the opening Hank needed.

He drove as a man possessed, finding holes where he could, but resorting to using the vehicle as a blunt instrument when all else failed. At first, the cars ahead were mostly empty or were soon to be, as the tentacles from god-knows-where recovered from their temporary setback and resumed a methodical reaping.

Once Hank made it to the middle of the bridge, out there with the lapping waters of the Bay on either, he met the second cause for the emptied and discarded vehicles along the roadway. He'd pulled the ambulance to the far right-hand lane, out on the other side was the water. At first, he mistook the spray and sprinkle of green brackish liquid against the windshield for rain. Yet when he peered up, he saw the early morning sun shining bright and oblivious in a sky that would otherwise be clear, if not for the winding columns of smoke. It was then he understood the water came from below. He struggled to imagine it, the normally placid, laconic waters churned up to such a degree that they sprayed the vehicles on the bridge above.

Amid this dribbling spray, another wet smacking sound, like a suction cup pulled from a glass surface and then reattached, caught Hank's ear.

Over and over, the sound repeated. The strange, unexpected noise reminded Hank of a troop of monkeys hooting and whimpering behind the glass at a zoo enclosure. It struck him as odd and unsettling. Despite his better nature's warning, he found he couldn't ignore the sound. Disregarding whatever best intentions he might've had as he took off across the bridge with an initial reckless abandon, Hank soon found his foot easing off the gas pedal.

It's recon, that's all. Gotta check the perimeter. Standard procedure...

Then, he caught a glimpse of the thick, chitinous crab claw, an appendage equal in size to a heavyweight prizefighter's fist, latching onto the top railing of the bridge. Then, another claw came down and the creature they belonged too pulled itself onto the Bridge. Its eyes were black, not like Hank's skin, but black like nothing at all. The black of those nightmares where Hank could feel himself falling into an abyss, only to wake, shaking, dripping sweat onto the sheets of the bed where he slept alone. The proportions of the creature's body were that of a man's, a powerful brick shithouse type of man, but a man, nonetheless. However, its shimmering skin, stretched like an oil spill over a head with no nose and gill slits on the sides, vibrated as the being sucked air in and out. Those features told a story of a being far removed from humanity.

Holy fuck.

Hank was grateful for the restraint he managed to demonstrate by only *thinking* his exclamation rather than shouting it to the Heavens. As the creature's bulbous lips pulled back to reveal jagged rows of teeth like broken glass and sewing needles, Hank had no desire to draw unwanted attention to himself. He slid down in his seat, twisting, squeezing, and contorting his body to tuck as much under the dashboard and steering wheel column as possible. It made for a tight fit, and he found his head still poked out a little at the top.

Hank hooded his eyelids, trying to cover as much of the whites of his eyes as he could. He whispered more prayers for Marcy and Abel, making pleas to a God he could hardly believe in.

He still wanted to make it home to his children. But given the creature he'd seen pulling its wet, squelching body over the railing and onto the bridge, he'd settle for the knowledge that his kids survived and that they would be *okay*.

When he felt those obsidian eyes turning toward him and caught the Fish-Man's head tilting in contemplation, Hank decided he'd seen enough. He closed his eyes. The *pok-pok-pok* sound of the creature's breathing echoed in the emptiness. Hank sat waiting, counting ragged, shallow breaths. He was certain he'd hear claws on the front windshield, that he'd come to and find the monster breaking through the thick pane. Soon, he believed, the Fish-Man would grab him by his neck or ears and rip his head off as the rest of him was defenestrated.

But at the end of that moment of certain doom, when Hank found his breathing continued uninterrupted, he willed his eyes open and found the road ahead clear of any bizarre piscine creature from the sea.

Then, from the far left-hand lane, a shrill cry rose and was countered by the *pok-pok-pok* of fishy lips smacking open and shut, open and shut. Like a choir singing in the round, more of the Fish-Men joined in. Hank realized he was hearing those beings as they worked their way through the cars ahead of the ambulance on the bridge. Soon, more crustacean claws scraped and scratched over the railing. Bursting from the waters below, each made a scrambling ascent onto the bridge.

"Fucking Fish-Men…" Hank said to no one.

Chapter 18

Hank muttered all the curses he knew. After all, as far as he was concerned, he was all he had out there in the middle of the Bay as far as a support system was concerned.

It surprised him to hear a familiar chuckle from the passenger seat. He knew he should keep watching the road and follow the progress of the Fish-Men's frenzied scramble across the lanes to extract the other survivors from their vehicles. And beyond that, he knew he ought to check on the progress of the titanic tentacles, chucking aside cars and trucks behind him. Hank sat there trapped between the two unnatural threats.

And yet, it was Darren's wry chuckle that hooked Hank, drawing him from his vigil. When he turned, he expected to find an empty seat waiting across the center console.

More fool him, he soon realized, especially given the tenor of the never-ending nightmare day in which he still somehow existed.

Darren was there. Flashing a shit-eating smile back at his old partner, but there, nonetheless. Hank's lip trembled, words caught in his throat. Something between a sob and a scream emerged instead.

"You're in a bad spot, huh, holmes?"

The voice Hank heard? That was Darren's voice. There was no echo of the raving cultists in his speech.

Hank responded without thinking; or perhaps it was better to say, he answered despite the maddening thoughts struggling to take hold of his mind. "Darren, quiet!" he whispered, his eyes darting to the windshield and the rampaging Fish-Men beyond.

This vision of Darren flickered when addressed directly, like a sci-fi hologram with someone's hand struck through, disrupting the light. Still, the grin on the EMT's face, even broken into a million smaller versions of itself, a smile made of smiles refracting over and over again, was very clearly *classic Darren*.

"What do you mean?! Am I talking too loud?! Are you afraid I'll alert the Fish-Men in front of us and the monster-sized tentacles behind us to your presence here?! Is that it?!"

Hank heard a single hiccupping laugh from the back, but he didn't need to turn around to know who it came from. Instead, he sat still, breathing slowly, waiting for the other visitor to lean in and make herself known.

In this way, he shared a moment of silence with these uncanny versions of his co-workers—his friends—now existing as something like ghosts, but then again, perhaps not something so easily defined. "Hey, Vic," Hank said finally.

"They're its parasites. The Fish-Men, I mean. Like bacteria. They followed the host down into the Earth's core and stayed there while it slumbered. They've fed and fattened themselves on its eons-long dreaming. But now it wakes, and they've become germs on a windy day, passing from the snot-riddled nostrils of the infected and seeking new hosts on which they can spread."

Vic delivered her speech with her usual quavering lilt, the way she got when it was clear to anyone who'd listen that she was past overdue for another shot of whisky. She needed the fiery brown and black liquid sliding down her throat to fill her with something like life. Hank felt sorry for her, still with the urge even after what he'd assumed was her death.

Darren picked up where Vic left off. "They won't find anyone worthy though. Not you or her or me. No one in those cars ahead of you either. The Host is perfection, the ideal sickness sustaining their unholy lives. You can't stay here forever, dude. They *will* find you..."

Hank studied the dashboard and the vehicle's controls, hunting for a solution that either wouldn't present itself or wouldn't let itself be perceived. Vic and Darren continued their commentary, spackling in the gaps of Hank's understanding. Giving him too much knowledge. Soon, this overflowing information became a new sickness oozing its way in through his eyes, nose, ears, and mouth. The sensation was akin to emerging screaming, crying from a mother's womb with the knowledge of loss. Not just the knowledge, but the complete and inescapable understanding of it.

"The tentacles are its many appendages..."

"No, less like appendages, more the equivalent of hairs on your arms and legs. They're a sign of its maturity."

"So many years, more than we can comprehend through our still-primitive reading of this planet's history, it's waited to be reborn, hibernating inside the shell of our hollowed-out Earth. Lava flows served as its amniotic fluid. The shifting of tectonic plates rocked it in its slumber. Until now, until...the big one."

The vision of Darren stretched toward the steering wheel. His chest flickered and exploded in a kaleidoscopic pattern of bloodstained clothing and skin frozen in a bleak eternity, drained of shadows. To at him head-on was like seeing a paper sketch of existence. Whatever this

Darren was, he made his point, tapping his fingers toward the controls for the siren and lights.

Vic whispered her confirmation before the query had even fully formed inside Hank's mind. "You have to do *something*, Hank. If you stay here and do nothing, they *will* find you and you *will* die. And that's not what you want. Is it? Don't you want to see your kids again? Isn't that why you're seeking counsel from the dead? If you don't believe us, should we bring *her* in as well?"

Even that slightest hint, the unspoken half-whisper of his wife's name, struck Hank harder than any blow. When he looked to Darren's phantasmagoric incarnation, still smiling in his seat, extended finger like a hook hand dangling above the steering column, Hank knew he'd find no other options presented to him.

As the decision was made, a shadow fell across the ambulance. Less than a half second later, Hank flipped the switch and activated the lights and siren. His head tilted up and he tried to gauge what might have caused the extensive darkness draping itself across the flashing white and red of the ambulance.

But the shouting and screaming came before he could understand. Vic and Darren, Marcy and Abel still waiting on the phone, Hank himself? *Those angry villagers outside of Kabul—No, not just angry at Uncle Sam, but angry...at me?* Hank couldn't tell who it was, and it didn't matter. All that mattered was what they commanded:

GO!

Chapter 19

The explosion of the tanker truck tumbling from the grasp of the redwood-thick tentacle as both vehicle and limb struck the bridge behind him propelled Hank and the ambulance forward. It was like a giant pool cue had struck the vehicle from behind. Hank's glowing, whining chariot ping-ponged off the remaining cars and trucks ahead, shearing the ambulance's mirrors away and scraping through its thick metal siding. Suddenly, the protective encasement Hank had enjoyed throughout the hellish day felt far less secure than he'd previously believed.

"I don't think your plan's working," the phantom Darren said.

Hank didn't get to remind his dead friend where the plan had actually come from.

While the lights and sirens had freed up a path before, thanks to his fellow humans acting out of habit and conditioning, pulling their cars and trucks to the side, avoiding contact with the flashing lights, signaling injury, disease, or even death, the Fish-Men had no such fears. As more of the aquatic humanoids clambered onto the bridge, the Fish-Men already present turned their attention to the fleeing ambulance.

Body after silver-skinned body went slipping and sliding, practically swimming through the air to get to Hank inside Ambulance 7. Crab claws struck the windshield, striking harder and harder, as more bodies pressed tight like sardines against the hood. "What am I supposed to do?" Hank asked.

But Darren and Vic weren't there any longer. They were gone, leaving with a fading whisper. "It's not so bad. Becoming a part of it. A part of something bigger than loneliness, fear, weakness, or grief. *Guilt*. It made us a part of something. Now we're the parasites, living off our host. And maybe that's enough for everyone. Even you..."

The statement was punctuated by a single claw bursting through the windshield. Chunks of glass flew inward, and Hank cried out in pain. Shards of glass pin-cushioned his arms and forehead. They strafed his cheeks. Stray slivers, like translucent hairs, appeared on his neck, inches away from ending his life. Then, the Fish-Man who'd made the hole dipped its head through the shattered remnants of the windshield, regarding Hank with cold, alien eyes. It looked at the driver the way Hank might've considered an ant intruding on a summer afternoon picnic.

Pok-pok-pok-pok.

There was no menace obvious in the creature's speech—if you could call those gasping intonations *language*. It seemed nothing more sophisticated than the commentary of a hand coming down on a housefly. Hank readjusted his grip on the steering wheel with his left hand, twisting the wheel from side to side, trying his damnedest to shake off any more of the monsters slamming against the sides of the ambulance like salmon striking the rocks in their uphill journey to the spawning grounds.

The Fish-Man on the hood pushed itself deeper inside the vehicle, bringing its slick metallic skin across the top of the dash. Its claw came down and pincered the cell phone Hank had placed there. For a moment, Hank swore he heard his kids crying, as though the claw itself had struck them. But the crunch and roar from the ruined device cut the exclamation short.

Pure adrenaline and breathless rage overtook him. Hank balled up his right hand into a fist and swung hard at the Fish-Man's head. His knuckles split open the slick skin on the Fish-Man's face, pulping the creature's visage. A black eye dripping with a viscous coating like roe was expelled from a socket. The eyeball and accompanying gore dripped onto the remains of the phone.

Hank wasn't going to stop there. His fist soon became a claw of his own, fingers hooking into the ruin of the creature's face. He squeezed tighter than he thought possible. The bottom half of the Fish-Man's jaw was wrenched down into the ambulance. Glass scratched and scraped, opening more wounds in the naked, seemingly genital-less body of Hank's attacker.

"Fuck you! Fuck you! Fuck you!"

Hank let go and brought his foot down on the brake. The Fish-Man and all its kin clamped onto the ambulance like barnacles on the waterlogged sides of a ship were stripped away with the sudden stop.

Before they could regroup, Hank hit the gas again. Wheels sharpened to guillotine blades by friction took some of their heads off as the ambulance raged forward. At that moment, vehicle and driver were one entity. A heat-seeking drone missile, unwavering from its target.

A hole in the bridge waited for them. Raging neon-green waters forced through the gap in geyser-like explosions. Hank was past the point of fear. Never mind how the jagged edges on either side of the normally flattened roadway appeared as though a gigantic creature had leaped up from the corrupted waters and snatched down a mouthful of steel and concrete. All Hank was concerned with was estimating distance and speed.

He'd driven a tank under enemy fire plenty of times in the desert. There, it was all abstract objectives, securing this and that, opening up pathways to democracy here or there. Or more typically, making sure whatever warlord was the most willing to play ball with the US government had the best set-up for his drug and sex trafficking operations care of Uncle Sam and the boys in tan camo. He'd learned to account for almost every contingency.

The ambulance creaked and whined, a good dog on last legs. Black smoke plumed from its hood.

Most of the medical equipment had already spilled out the back of the vehicle. If there was anyone left to follow Hank's trail, they'd have discovered the remnants of healers in his wake. Hank was never an EMT, never a medic. Hell, he'd fallen short of getting his Eagle badge in Boy Scouts because he'd never completed his First Aid merit badge.

Hank was no healer.

"I'm a driver," he said.

There was no one, not a thing, left to answer. But that didn't stop him from repeating himself, bellowing his declaration to the curdled and yellowed heavens.

"I'M A DRIVER!"

What else was he supposed to do?

Picking up speed, fires sparked against the bridge until flames coated the sides of the ambulance like the wings of a demon on heavy metal album art. The black rubber of the steering wheel turned a gummy, sticky mess against Hank's palms. And as fast as he felt the pain, he screamed through it, shoving the worst of it down into the deepest, darkest parts of himself.

He figured it for the best. After all, he'd already taken so much of those worst parts and let them be released, allowing them to see the sunlight despite earlier assurances he'd made that they would be suppressed until he died.

'Til death do we part.

Dodging the remaining cars, snapping claws, and slapping tentacles, Hank operated on instinct alone. That is, until he noticed the Fish-Men gathered by the edge of the hole nearest to the approaching ambulance. They appeared to have grown tired of seeking prey among the fleeing humans and had instead opted to lasso and pull down one of the massive tentacles—the appendages *Vic* and *Darren* told him were a part of something else, something bigger than anything Hank could possibly understand.

And they would know. After all, the tentacles had claimed them, made them a part of whatever this other greater *entity* was.

"Look over and you'll see. Right there to the side, it's almost fully emerged from within the earth. Its body fills the bay."

It was Livia who spoke the words.

Hank's tears emerged unbidden. They sizzled when warmed by the intense heat inside the car. And Hank couldn't even lift his burned hands from the wheel to wipe them away. Even as the glass from the windshield was driven deeper into his head, his entire body shook along to the rattling of the vehicle.

Ahead, the Fish-Men stopped devouring the tentacle. They turned as one to acknowledge the banshee's siren wail came from the ambulance.

The black pools of their eyes blended together into one massive empty hole, an ebon mirror in which Hank saw the darkest, most distorted version of himself. Consequently, he wasn't surprised when the Fish-Men's lips quivered and their mouths emitted a rattling, choking cry that was as close as they might come to a scream, nor was he shocked when they rose from their sinewy haunches and fled from the incoming vehicle, diving through the hole in the bridge to the polluted waters below.

In that moment, Hank was far more of monster than even those strange ravenous creatures from the deep.

With his path cleared, Hank finally spoke to his wife. "I'm sorry," he said, "Sorry, I won't look. Sorry, I won't see it. I just...I can't. I never should've told you what happened over there in the desert. Never should've told you what I saw. They were two kids. Playing too close to the tank treads."

"That's what you do," she answered. "You don't look. You never see."

Hank gave her the last word. Because he felt he owed her that much. Deep down, he believed she was right and that there was nothing he could do to change.

The ambulance's ruined, burning front wheels struck the narrowest part of the detached tentacle. Momentum carried the vehicle forward and Hank's cry marked his Herculean efforts to keep it straight and true. He rode the incline of the tentacle as if he was on a ramp.

Up and up he went until he reached the end, and there was only the hole in the road and below that a swirling, angry whirlpool of diseased waters.

Hank's ass come off the seat. His hands tore free from the steering wheel, leaving his palms pink and raw like spoiled hamburger meat.

He clasped those hands together, as though in prayer. But he couldn't imagine a God worthy of his pleas.

Chapter 20

The ambulance landed on its front wheels at the other side of the bridge. The vehicle struck hard enough to crack one of Hank's molars. For a moment, it appeared the vehicle was toppling forward, preparing to flip over and show its undercarriage. Hank was certain it was inevitable that the wheels would spin like a turtle mishandled and left kicking, kicking, trying desperately to right itself.

His charred and bleeding hands returned to the steering wheel, and he pulled back on it. As though he could defy the laws of physics. "Come on," he said, "Come on, come on."

Metal shrieked. Filling his ears, filling his entire being.

Lucky him, the back wheels struck the ground, and the ambulance landed upright, squared, and as intact as could be hoped for. Hank's laugh came out loud and long. Even with the stink of carrion rot blasting through the shattered windshield, he chuckled heartily, his cheeks shaking.

Retaining control of the broken-down vehicle was akin to riding a bucking bronco at the rodeo, but in this particular case, the rider had already been beaten by a mob and thrown out of a high-rise beforehand.

At least, the flames were out. The once white ambulance was now a far darker shade of black than Hank.

"C'mon, just a little more," he begged. His jittery feet tested the gas, revving the engine slightly. When he found forward motion was still possible, *though not exactly easy*, he elected to give it all he had once again.

However much that might be...

Slamming the pedal to the floor, Hank took Ambulance 7 off the Bay Bridge. With flashing lights and the hissing wail of a siren, they blew past a road sign. Bent and twisted, marred by deep scratches, it offered Hank a "WELCOME TO OAKLAND."

It'd been hours since Hank checked on the state of things in his city.

It was time enough for aftershocks to roll across the Bay. The crumbled buildings, ruined streets, and stray body parts glimpsed amid the rubble, everything that'd come to characterize the final portions of Hank's journey through San Francisco now marked its sister city. "At least there's no tentacles here. Yet..."

Hank spoke the words aloud, far past the point of feeling the need to keep his delirious thoughts to himself. The elevated BART lines were elevated no more. Sparking metal rails and concrete pillars marked the splintered ruins. Hank imagined the underground portions of the train line crushed under the unforgiving weight of the earth brought low.

On a normal day, when his shift ended, he'd take the train back to Marcy and Abel, walking the final few blocks home.

In those rare moments when he'd go out for a post-work drink in San Francisco with Vic and Darren, Hank would often hear tech bros, the ones who'd taken over San Francisco, telling each other horror stories, urban legends \ heard through the grapevine about the dangers of a life in Oakland. They'd cluck like worried hens about how violent it was supposed to be. How crime ridden.

Hank always made sure to catch their eyes and lift an eyebrow. As if to say, "Oh, you mean it's too *Black,* don't you?" His look alone usually shut them up and resulted in the offenders moving along down the bar.

When Hank went home to Oakland, he never once worried that something bad would happen to him.

Whenever he'd mention it, Darren would laugh and say, "Yeah, but you're a big motherfucker, my dude."

Enclosed in the brittle burnt metal of the ambulance, Hank didn't feel all that big as he worked it through the empty streets of Oakland. At the very least, he was grateful for the quiet. There weren't the marauding bands or chanting cultists on this side of the bridge. The scenes in Oakland, all smoke-filled and reeking of corruption as they were, remained set-pieces from a disaster film. Brutal, devastating, and heart-wrenching. But without the feeling of driving through a waking nightmare as Hank had left behind in San Francisco.

He focused on driving, taking it slow. He feared pressing the pedal down any further might cause the vehicle to shudder and collapse. And he didn't believe he'd be too far behind.

Leaving the horrors across the Bay out of sight, out of mind, Hank refused to look back the way he'd come. The blood from his facial wounds clotted around the shards. The glass was fused to his skin thanks to the extreme heat he'd passed through. His injuries ached at last. More tears fell unbidden from his eyes.

As far as Hank was concerned, they were tears of joy and triumph. Even with the nearby street signs bent and mangled, there was no way he'd get lost along the way home. Nothing could stop him from reaching his children.

The barricade, stretched across the road, tried to tell a different story.

Chapter 21

The surviving people of Oakland had a good reason for being out of sight as Hank drove Ambulance 7 through the emptied and devastated streets. All those people weren't lost, trapped under rubble, sheltering in place, or waiting for rescue. Oh no. Far from it.

Instead, every man, woman, and child who'd made it through the devastating earthquake had gathered together in one place.

And they'd all tied or chained themselves to a makeshift barricade stretched across Telegraph Avenue, one of the main thoroughfares through the East Bay.

To call it a barricade was putting it lightly. Stretched across the road, it would make for a breathtaking feat of civil engineering if viewed in any other light than that of the day's insanity. Hank couldn't imagine what the rest of the country—hell, the rest of the world—might have to say about the human-studded structure and every other bizarre occurrence he'd witnessed since the Earth began falling apart under his feet.

Funny, how there haven't been planes in the sky. No helicopters either. Nothing since all this started. Where's the rest of the world? Do they just not want to help anymore?

Hank certainly understood the impulse if that was the case.

The structure's assemblers had pulled together cyclone fencing, concrete blocks, bricks, steel beams, and other remnants of the many obliterated buildings along the streets, to form the monstrosity covering both lanes and even the sidewalk on either side. The whole construction was long and wide enough to block any viable alternative paths that Hank might use to circumvent it. Worse still than the jagged, junkyard aesthetic of the piece was the addition of the people tied up at regular intervals. The resulting outer layer of flesh and bone and blood completed the mise-en-scène.

Thick wet ropes and rusted chains were pulled taut and looped around arms and legs. Some restraints bit into the flesh of necks or across foreheads. If any of those chained to the barricade strained against their binds, it wasn't because they longed to be free. But rather it was because they were *singing*. They made for an ecstatic, exuberant choir.

Their chanting greeted Hank like a tidal wave crashing onto normally dry land, hitting distressing notes, the same ones as he'd heard on the radio. Same as he'd heard from the Bleeding Man and the cultists leaping from the overpass to a splattered, pulped finish on the streets of San Francisco. It was a song that should've been more than familiar to Hank by that point in his day of horrors.

And perhaps it was.

But that didn't mean he had to like it.

"SHUT UP!"

Hank had forgotten about his windshield being knocked out. So, he was a bit taken aback when the chanters stopped mid-drone. Hanging from the concrete and metal of the barricade, they regarded him with bloodshot eyes. Someone's mouth opened, lips curling to form words. As if there was a simple, straightforward explanation not just for why they hung there and sang. But for everything.

Before the answer was given, the would-be speaker had their face pushed out the back of their exploded head, driven hard against the barricade by the impact of the ambulance crashing into it at full speed.

Hank pressed the pedal without thinking about anything besides his children. He didn't allow himself to consider consequences. His ambulance shot forward, flying straight and true through the blockade. When he hit resistance and the vehicle's smashed and twisted front would longer make forward progress, he backed up, then rammed through again. Over and over.

Some on the barricade—those well and truly dedicated to the cause—attempted to resume their chanting. Even with metal twisting and bones cracking before him, Hank found he could understand some of what the mangled bodies referred to. Their words told of ancient creatures pre-dating the emergence of multi-celled organisms as science understood them, of buried horrors, of cataclysms that last forever occurring in pockets of reality that no one but the suffering could access, and of new, emergent worlds stripped and cleansed of peace and hope.

Their efforts to deny reality, to keep singing in the face of wanton slaughter, turned to naught as Hank shoved his ambulance through to the other side of the barricade. Debris flew back into his face. More cuts   and   gouges   opened   across   his body.

But he no longer cared. Even when he heard the screams and cries of children just like his, maybe even younger than his, Hank could find no escape hatch, no opportunity to back away from the choice he'd made.

He'd vowed to make it home. He'd promised he'd make it back for his children. And there was no way he'd abandon that goal with the finish line so close. Close enough so he could feel it, the sensation imbuing his worn limbs with new life, new energy.

The bodies wrecked against the smoking hull of the ambulance were a price he was more than willing to pay. There was no one left to command him or to offer advice. No one to tell him if what he did was right or wrong. All he had left was Marcy and Abel.

When the time came, Hank would ask his children for absolution.

And forgiveness.

He'd let their hugs and kisses wash away his sins.

Chapter 22

Ambulance 7 sputtered and died before the ruins of the apartment complex. There was no more juice to be squeezed from its engine. There was no *one last time* to press the pedal to the floor and accelerate another inch, let alone another block. It was well and truly dead.

But it didn't matter. Hank's journey was finished. Even as torn flesh and severed body parts sizzled on the mangled front grill of the vehicle, its driver shoved his door open, allowing his body to slide off the seat and down to the ground. The impact was sudden, driving chipped teeth through his tongue. The swollen pink and purple muscle was torn, and dark blood filled his mouth.

As Hank stood, he held in a scream that had seemed inevitable since his journey home began. He didn't want to scare his children, didn't know how close they might be under the rubble. Even as he put a hand against the vehicle to steady himself and the heated metal cooked his flesh, he kept silent. Blood and sick spewed from his mouth with a hiccup. It dribbled past his lips like he was a newborn overfed on milk.

His hands moved to his knees, and he doubled over, spitting out strands of foaming red saliva. His ravaged face was reflected in the silvered surface of a gasoline puddle. There was no time for revulsion, even though the bloodied, blackened, glass-shard-studded thing staring back from the shimmering surface was a creature of nightmares.

He closed his eyes, then stood straight and tall. When he opened his eyes, lightning crashed above his head, balls of white-hot energy annotating a sky the same hue as dried blood. Again, Hank refused to turn around and check back the way he'd come.

There was only *forward*.

"Kids!"

He waited a moment after his first cry, then took a step forward and repeated himself. "Kids! Marcy! Abel!"

He knew they had to be close. They'd told him they were in the lobby.

And that was real. It was a real call. It had to have been.

Refusing to let doubt crawl in, Hank lunged for the wreckage, putting his body amid the ruins of home. Some combination of adrenaline, grief, and rage at the insanity surrounding him, imbued Hank with strength far beyond his norm. Bricks and glass, plaster chunks and concrete, all flew backward as he tossed them aside and dug down into the heart of the disaster site.

He kept up a steady stream of shouting, hoping to hear the matching cry from his kids. The attempted rescue effort made for a Herculean task and Hank was the demi-god on his last legs, at the end of his labors, trying to push through one last time for love.

"Marcy! Abel! Answer me!"

He caught the sound of gravel shifting... indicating a pillar shaken loose as a result of his digging. He moved quickly to shove it aside like a tackling dummy, ensuring it fell away from where he estimated his children to be. The collision drove a storm-cloud grey piece of rebar through his shoulder. The piece exited his body just as quickly when Hank pulled away from the pillar and resumed his search in full force.

Fat dollops of blood spilled down Hank's tattered shirt, adding to the sticky, coppery coating he'd gained on his way home.

Then, someone coughed.

Hank froze. Waited.

Another cough followed. A tiny, strident whine.

It was the most beautiful thing Hank had heard in years.

Far, far better than tears and despairing wails. Better than his own voice fumbling nervously through a confession of all the terrible things he'd ever done.

"I drove the tank and ran over those kids, Liv. We were escorting some private security guys, hush-hush thing, and we couldn't be caught. So they told me to drive and keep driving... Please don't turn away from me, please I need to tell someone. You're it. You're my rock. You can take it...right?"

"Daddy?"

One word came like another whisper. Something subtle as though he'd heard it in a dream. But that was enough. Enough to hook its barbs into Hank and pull him back to the work at hand. He flung more debris to the side, stretching and straining his muscles.

Finally, smaller hands closed around his forearm. Fingers pinched his skin. Then, he saw eyes staring up at him. Those eyes were as gorgeous as any rare jewels one might ever get a chance to see.

"I got you," he told them. "Daddy's got you."

The remaining work was slow. Tedious. The savagery of his initial efforts was replaced by the delicate, precise removal of the surrounding wreckage. He worked like he was in the middle of an intense game of Jenga, one where the tower's collapse would mean ruin and heartbreak with no second chances. At last, his children were freed from their prison and returned to the light of the world above.

Marcy held on tight to her brother. Through it all, she'd remained his protector. Their faces were ashen, so it looked as though their skeletons were being pushed out from the inside, breaking through their skin. The girl's braided pigtails had come undone. The red plastic baubles that the babysitter had tied them with sat smashed against the top of her head. It looked as though a traffic light was broken there. Caught in the glow of the heat lightning rampaging overhead, the shards became a flashing warning signal.

Danger! Danger! Danger!

Abel's tiny afro was an unkempt mountain of curls above his head. His pants were wet and dark. The pungent odor of urine was impossible for even Hank's destroyed nose to miss.

But for all that, Hank saw cause for celebration. they were free. And that's all that mattered as far as Hank was concerned.

He pulled them both close. Encountering his touch, they fell against him. All three squeezed tight, as though they might become one single entity with the slightest effort.

Inseparable.

But Marcy pulled away from the shared embrace first. She leaned over to the side, putting her mouth closer to her daddy's ear. Her rosebud lips whispered breathless words, vibrating inside Hank's skull.

"Look, Daddy," she said.

Then, Abel whispered too. Speaking in a lisp he still hadn't overcome. "Wook, Daddy."

The next breath Hank was meant to take, got snagged in his windpipe. A solid, constricting effort meant couldn't answer beyond a wheeze. High-pitched and frightened.

Look. Look. Look. Look.

Over and over again, it repeated until their request became a command. Soon, Hank found he had no words of protest to match them.

They were his children after all. His entire world. He'd do anything for them.

Right?

So, he turned and looked back the way he'd come, back toward the Bay.

With all of the buildings destroyed on either side of those poisoned waters, there was no way to miss what rose from the depths of the Earth. A colossal behemoth towered above the wastelands. A green-hued titan casting blackened eyes down on chaos. Tentacles descended from a void where its mouth might be. Muscles like a mountain range glowed with otherworldly radioactivity. There was so much of the entity to be seen that to look upon it meant nothing else could attract the observer's attention away from the act of observation.

Blood leaked afresh from all Hank's wounds. The thick serum spilled from behind his eyes. Combined with unbidden tears, the taste of pennies and saltwater passed his lips. The entity's body was coated in a layer of tentacles, those same appendages that had snatched away Darren, Vic, and so many others.

Even me, even here at the end.

Looking up at this being and watching its slow steady movements from down at his place on the ruined Earth, Hank experienced something like what the astronauts would go through when looking at the planet from outer space. Suddenly, he was struck dumb by the understanding of his place in the universe. "Nothing...we're nothing," he said. "All for nothing."

Hank grew smaller and smaller the more he watched the monster pulsing with energy from beyond the stars. For him, there was only this being, this Host, this undeniable true *Big One*, taking up all of his attention.

He missed the exact moment when the children melted away, transformed into a gray sludge that ran through his fingers. They became the stuff of nightmares, the dust left over when a sleeper finally awakens.

Acknowledgements

As I've mentioned time and time again, it's quite rare for a book to come together with no outside help or assistance. I'm sure it must happen sometimes.

But this is *not* one of those times.

To that end, I must give credit to all those who've helped to bring *The Big One* to your physical and/or virtual bookshelves.

First, thanks to Tony Anuci for stepping in and stepping up to help bring the book to life. Tony's enthusiasm for the indie horror publishing scene is palpable in every book put out byAnuci Press. I was so pleased that this manuscript resonated with him and that he was onboard with putting this book out the way I want it presented.

I must also thank Mia Dalia for providing this connection to Tony and the press. Mia is a wonderfully evocative writer herself. If you haven't had a chance to read her work, I recommend fixing that post-haste.

Thanks also to Justin Talarski who originally saw the potential in the manuscript as a release for another publisher. While it didn't work out in that incarnation, I am grateful for the initial support and enthusiasm. Sometimes getting that little extra boost from knowing someone else is vibing with your ideas is all we need as writers to keep going, to keep pushing forward with projects.

Speaking of things working out, I must thank the divine cover artist/designer Lynne Hansen for her stellar work on the cover design of *The Big* One. When I first got to see Lynne's work on the cover, I was blown away. It had (and still has for that matter) everything I'd ever hoped for in a *The Big One* cover.

Tentacles? Check.

Explosions? Check.

I'm glad we were able to secure Lynne's services for the cover design and can't imagine the book without her keenly diabolical artistic eye.

Finally, thank you, readers. With this project, I had the wild idea to mess around and see what might happen if some big-budget action director like Michael Bay tried to make a Lovecraftian horror tale that took place in the middle of some IMAX-sized natural disaster action tentpole flick. Thank you, you absolute maniacs, for agreeing to go along with this bonkers premise. I certainly hope you're closing this book with a smile on your face. And maybe that you're also shaking your head and wondering just what the hell is wrong with me...or you.

About the Author

Patrick Barb is an author of weird, dark, and horrifying tales, currently living (and trying not to freeze to death) in Saint Paul, Minnesota. His published works include his debut sci-fi/horror novel *Abducted*, the dark fiction collections *The Children's Horror* and *Pre-Approved for Haunting*, the novellas *The Big One*, *The Nut House*, *Night of the Witch-Hunter*, and *JK-LOL*, as well as the novelette *Helicopter Parenting in the Age of Drone Warfare*. In addition, he is the editor and publisher of the anthology *And One Day We Will Die: Strange Stories Inspired by the Music of Neutral Milk Hotel*, and runs the monthly interview column "Your Favorite Author's Favorite Author" in *Shortwave Magazine*. His 2023 short story "The Scare Groom" was selected for *Best Horror of the Year Volume 16*. Visit him at patrickbarb.com.